THE PHANTOM OF THE TEMPLE

In the remote western border district of Lan-fang, separated from the vast Tartar steppes of Central Asia by only a boundary river, Judge Dee faces and solves one of the most frightening cases of his long career.

Outside the east city gate, on a wooded hill, stands a centuries-old Buddhist temple. There the phantom stalks, and there also a series of brutal murders are committed. Judge Dee's inquiry into them is complicated by a mysterious dying message from a young girl called Jade, and by the theft of a large sum of gold from an Imperial Treasurer.

Judge Dee Mysteries Available from Chicago:

THE PHANTOM
OF THE TEMPLE

A Judge Dee Mystery

by

ROBERT VAN GULIK

**With *nine illustrations*
*drawn by the author in Chinese style***

THE UNIVERSITY OF CHICAGO PRESS

Published by arrangement with Scribner,
A Division of Simon & Schuster Inc.

The University of Chicago Press, Chicago 60637
© Robert van Gulik, 1966
All rights reserved. Originally published 1966
University of Chicago Press edition 1995
Printed in the United States of America
16 15 14 13 12 11 10 09 08 07   2 3 4 5 6

ISBN-13: 978-0-226-84877-8 (paper)
ISBN-10: 0-226-84877-9 (paper)

Library of Congress Cataloging-in-Publication Data
Gulik, Robert Hans van, 1910–1967.
    The phantom of the temple / by Robert van Gulik ; with
    nine illustrations drawn by the author in Chinese style. —
    University of Chicago Press ed.
        p.   cm. — (A Judge Dee mystery)
    1. Dee Jen-Djieh (Fictitious character)—Fiction.
    2. China— History—T'ang dynasty, 618–907—Fiction.
    3. Judges—China—Fiction.   I. Title.   II. Series: Gulik,
    Robert Hans van, 1910–1967.   Judge Dee mystery.
    PR9130.9.G8P48   1995
    823'.914—dc20   95-24390
                                                                              CIP

DRAMATIS PERSONAE

Note that in Chinese the surname—here printed
in capitals—precedes the personal name

Main characters

DEE Jen-djieh	in 670 A.D. magistrate of Lan-fang, a district on the western frontier of the Tang Empire
HOONG Liang	his trusted adviser and Sergeant of the tribunal
MA Joong	one of his lieutenants

Others

Seng-san	a vagrant ruffian
Lao-woo	his brother
Ah-liu	his friend
The Monk	head of the beggars
Mrs CHANG	Abbess of the Temple of the Purple Clouds
Spring Cloud	her maidservant
Tala	a Buddhist sorceress
LEE Mai	banker and owner of a gold- and silver-shop
LEE Ko	his brother, a painter
WOO Tsung-jen	retired prefect
Mrs WOO	his wife
YANG Mou-te	a student

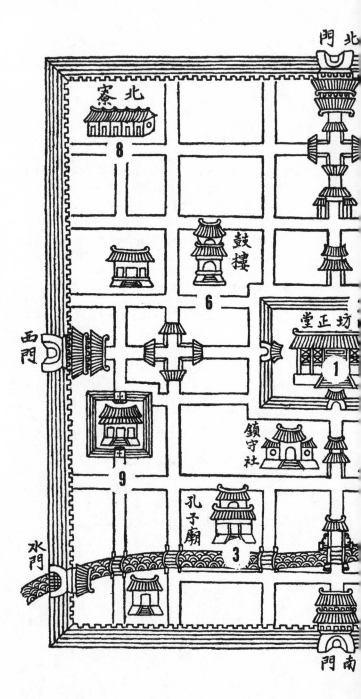

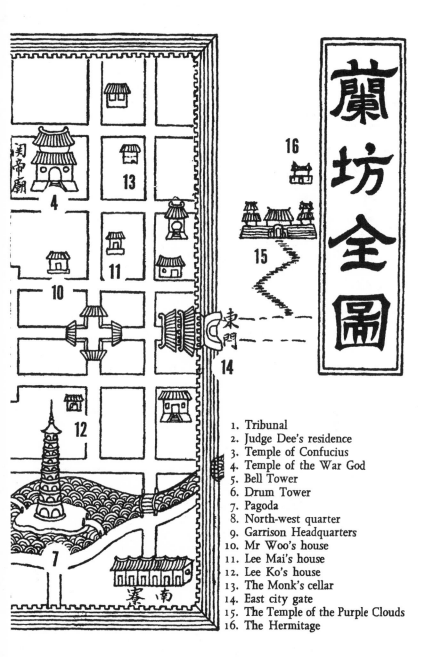

蘭坊全圖

1. Tribunal
2. Judge Dee's residence
3. Temple of Confucius
4. Temple of the War God
5. Bell Tower
6. Drum Tower
7. Pagoda
8. North-west quarter
9. Garrison Headquarters
10. Mr Woo's house
11. Lee Mai's house
12. Lee Ko's house
13. The Monk's cellar
14. East city gate
15. The Temple of the Purple Clouds
16. The Hermitage

ILLUSTRATIONS

A sketch map of Lan-fang appears on pages vi–vii.
The maid's floor-plan of the deserted temple is found
on page 140.

I

She stared in silence at the thing lying on the rim of the old well. Not a breeze stirred in the hot, damp air that hung heavily in the dark temple garden. A few almond blossoms came fluttering down from the spreading branches overhead, very white in the light of the lantern. And whiter still when they stuck to the bloodstains on the weatherbeaten stones.

Clutching her wide robe to her bosom, she said to the tall man standing beside her, 'Throw it into the well too! It'll be quite safe; this old well hasn't been used for years. I don't think anybody even knows of its existence.'

He cast an anxious look at her pale, expressionless face, placed the lantern on the pile of boulders and broken bricks beside the well and loosened his neckcloth with impatient jerks.

'I want to play it double safe, you see. I shall wrap it up and . . .' Noticing that his voice sounded very loud in the deserted temple garden, he continued in a whisper, '. . . bury it among the trees behind the temple. The drunken fool is sound asleep and nobody else'll be about for it's past midnight.'

She watched dispassionately as he wrapped the severed head up in his neckcloth. His fingers trembled so violently that he had difficulty in tying the ends.

1

'I can't help it!' he muttered defensively. 'It . . . it's getting too much for me. How . . . how did you do it? Twice, and so deftly . . .'

She shrugged her shoulders.

'You have to know about the spacing of the joints,' she replied with indifference. Then she bent over the rim of the well. Thick clusters of ivy had overgrown the mouldering wood of the broken crossbar and long, rank streamers hung down into the dark depths, clinging to the half-decayed rope that once had a pitcher attached to it. Something stirred in the dense foliage of the towering old trees. Again there was a thin shower of white blossoms. A few dropped on her hand. They felt cold, like snow. She drew her hand back and shook them off. Then she said, slowly, 'Last winter, this garden was all white with snow. All white . . .' Her voice trailed off.

'Yes,' he said eagerly. 'Yes! Down in the city it was beautiful too. Icicles hung from the eaves of the pagoda in the lotus lake like so many small bells.' He wiped his moist, hot face and added, 'How clean the frosty air was; I remember that in the morning . . .'

'Don't remember,' she interrupted coldly. 'Forget! Think only of the future. For now we shall be able to get it. All of it. Let's go now, and get it out of there.'

'Now?' he exclaimed, aghast. 'Just after . . .' Seeing her contemptuous look, he resumed quickly: 'I am dog-tired, I tell you. Really!'

'Tired? You always boast about your strength!'

'But there isn't any hurry any more, is there? We can go and take it, any time we like. And we . . .'

'I happen to be in a hurry. But I suppose it'll keep. What is one night?'

He looked at her unhappily. She was withdrawing into

2

herself again, away from him. And his desire for this woman was so poignant that it hurt him.

'Why can't you belong to me, to me alone?' he pleaded. 'You know I'll do anything you want. I proved it, I . . .'

He broke off, for he saw that she was not listening. She was staring up at an open space between the branches, strewn with white blossoms. The tops of the two three-storeyed towers stood out clearly against the evening sky. They flanked the main hall of the temple, in perfect symmetry.

II

Early the next morning the heavy hot air still hung over the city of Lan-fang. When Judge Dee came back to his private office from his morning walk he noticed with dismay that his cotton robe, drenched with sweat, was sticking to his broad shoulders. He took the small wooden box from his sleeve and put it on his desk. Then he went to the clothes-box in the corner. After he had changed into a clean summer robe of blue cotton, he pushed the window open and looked outside. His burly lieutenant Ma Joong was crossing the paved courtyard of the tribunal compound, carrying a whole roasted pig on his shoulders. He was humming a song. It sounded thin and eerie in the empty yard.

The judge closed the window and sat down behind his desk, littered with papers. Rubbing his face, he reflected that he too ought to feel happy on this special day. His eyes strayed to the small ebony box he had put on the end of the desk. The round disc of green jade that decorated its smooth black cover shone with a dull gleam. When taking his morning walk he had seen the box in the shop window of a curio-dealer down town and bought it at once. For the jade disc was carved into the stylized shape of the character for 'long life', which made the box eminently suited for today's occasion. There was no earthly reason why he should be feeling out of sorts. He must take himself in hand. The dreary life in this remote frontier district was making him restive. He ought not to give in to these occasional moods of depression.

With a determined gesture he cleared a space on the desk in front of him by pushing a bulky dossier aside and clapped his hands to summon a clerk. Breakfast would settle the queasy feeling in his stomach. The heat had something to do with it too, probably. He picked up his large fan of crane-feathers. Leaning back in his armchair of carved blackwood, he slowly fanned himself.

The door opened and a frail old man came shuffling inside. He was clad in a long blue gown, a small black skull-cap covered his grey head. He wished the judge a good morning and carefully placed the breakfast tray on the side table. As he began to move the teapot and the small plates with salted fish and vegetables to the desk, Judge Dee said with a smile:

'You should have let the clerk bring my breakfast, Hoong! Why should you trouble to?'

'I was passing by the kitchen anyway, sir. I saw there that Ma Joong has found at the meat shop the largest roasted pig I have ever seen!'

'Yes, that'll be the main dish tonight. Here, give me that teapot, I can help myself! Sit down, Hoong!'

But the old man shook his head. He quickly poured the judge a cup of hot tea and placed the bowl of fragrant steaming rice in front of him. Only then did he sit down on the low stool in front of the desk. He had covertly observed Judge Dee's drawn face. Having been a retainer of the Dee family ever since Judge Dee's boyhood, he knew his master's every mood. Taking up his chopsticks, the judge said:

5

'I didn't sleep too well last night, Hoong. This hearty breakfast will set me up again.'

'It's a trying climate here in Lan-fang,' Sergeant Hoong remarked in his dry, precise voice. 'A cold, wet winter, then this hot, clammy summer, with sudden cold blasts coming in from the desert plain across the border. You must keep fit, sir. One easily catches a nasty cold here.' He sipped his tea, carefully holding up his long frayed moustache with his left hand. After he had set his cup down he resumed, 'Yesterday evening I saw a light burning here long past midnight, sir. I hope that no important case has cropped up?'

The judge shook his head.

'No, there was nothing special. Nothing much has happened here, Hoong, after I restored law and order, half a year ago. A few cases of manslaughter down town, a theft or two, that's about all! Our work consists mainly of the ordinary administrative routine. Registration of births, marriages and deaths, the settling of minor disputes, tax-collecting. . . . Very peaceful. Too peaceful, I nearly said!' He laughed, but the old man noticed that it was rather a forced laugh. 'Sorry, Hoong,' the judge resumed quickly. 'I am getting a bit stale, that's all. I'll get over that soon enough. What is much more serious: I am worried about my wives. Life is very dreary for them, out here. They hardly have any interesting lady-friends in this small provincial town, and there is little amusement. No good theatrical performances, no places for pleasant outings. . . . And the Tartar influence is still so strong that even our Chinese seasonal feasts are observed here with little circumstance. That is why I am glad of this little celebration for my First Lady tonight.' He shook his head and ate for a while in silence. After he had put down his chopsticks he leaned back in his chair.

6

'You asked about last night, Hoong. Well, while rummaging in the archives of this tribunal, I found the dossier dealing with that notorious unsolved case of theft that occurred here. The theft of the Imperial Treasurer's gold.'

'Why take an interest in that case, sir? It dates from last year. From before you assumed office here in Lanfang!'

'Exactly. It happened on the second day of the eighth month of the year of the Snake, to be precise. But unsolved cases always interest me, Hoong. Whether old or new!'

The old man nodded slowly.

'I remember reading in the Imperial Gazette about that theft, when we were still in Poo-yang. It created quite a stir in official circles. The Treasurer passed through here on his way to the Khan of the Tartars across the frontier. His orders were to purchase a team of the best Tartar horses from the Khan, for the Imperial stables. He was carrying fifty heavy gold bars.'

'Yes, Hoong. The gold was stolen during the night, and replaced by lead. The thief was never found and—'

There was a knock on the door. Ma Joong came in and said with a broad grin, 'I bought the most magnificent roasted pig, sir!'

'I saw you bring it in, Ma Joong. We have only one guest tonight, a lady-friend of my wives, and she is a vegetarian. So there'll be plenty of roasted pig left for all of you. Sit down. I was talking with the sergeant about the theft of the Treasurer's gold last year.'

His tall lieutenant sat down heavily on the second stool.

'An Imperial Treasurer is supposed to know how to

guard the government gold entrusted to him,' he remarked indifferently. 'That's what he's paid for! Yes, I remember the case. Wasn't the fellow summarily dismissed from the service?'

'He was,' Judge Dee replied. 'The thief was not found and the gold never recovered. Yet the case was investigated with painstaking care.' He laid his hand on the dossier in front of him and went on: 'This is a very instructive record, Ma Joong, well worth a close study. The magistrate first interrogated the captain and the soldiers of the Treasurer's escort. He reasoned that, since such large transports of gold are a closely guarded official secret, and since only the Treasurer himself was supposed to know the purpose of his mission, the thief must have been an insider. Another fact also pointed in that direction. The Treasurer's luggage consisted of three leather boxes, of exactly the same size, shape and colour, the lids of all three being secured by identical padlocks. The only distinguishing mark was that one side of the box containing the gold was slightly cracked. Now, only that box was opened. The two other boxes, which contained the Treasurer's clothes and other personal effects, were not tampered with at all. That's why the magistrate began by suspecting the Treasurer's suite.'

'On the other hand,' Sergeant Hoong observed, 'the thief replaced the gold by lead. Evidently because he hoped that the Treasurer would discover the loss only when he opened the box much later, after his arrival in barbarian territory. This clearly points to an outsider. All insiders know the official rule that a carrier of government gold has to verify it is intact every night before he goes to bed, and every morning as soon as he has got up.'

Judge Dee nodded.

'Quite true. However, my predecessor considered the

8

lead as a clever touch, added by the thief to suggest that the theft had been committed by an outsider.'

Ma Joong had risen and walked over to the window. Having searched the empty courtyard with his eyes, he said with a frown:

'I wonder what that lazy headman is doing! He should be taking his constables through their morning drill!' Seeing Judge Dee's annoyed look, he went on quickly, 'Sorry, sir! But now that Chiao Tai and Tao Gan have left for the capital to discuss the reduction of our garrison, I have to watch the constables and guards all by myself.' He sat down again and asked, eager to show his interest, 'Didn't the thief leave any clues?'

'None,' the judge replied curtly. 'The guest room occupied by the Treasurer in our tribunal here has only one door and one window, as you know. The door was guarded all night long by four soldiers, sitting in the corridor outside. The thief gained entrance by the window. He tore one of the paper panes, pushed his hand through, and somehow or other picked the lock that secured the crossbar.'

Sergeant Hoong had pulled the thick dossier over to him and was leafing through it. He looked up and said, shaking his head, 'Yes, the magistrate took all the measures indicated. When it had been established that the Treasurer's suite was beyond suspicion, he had all the professional thieves in the city rounded up, and also all the receivers of stolen goods. Moreover, he—'

'He made one mistake, Hoong,' Judge Dee interrupted. 'Namely that he limited his investigation to this district of Lan-fang.'

'Why shouldn't he?' Ma Joong asked. 'The theft was committed right here, wasn't it?'

The judge sat up straight.

9

'It was indeed. But it must have been prepared elsewhere, before the Treasurer arrived here in Lan-fang. Therefore I would have begun by instituting thorough inquiries in Tong-kang, our neighbouring district, over on the other side of the mountains. The Treasurer stayed there overnight as well. Someone must have learned somehow or other that he was carrying a small fortune, and that it was kept in the box marked by the cracked leather. That precious information travelled ahead of the Treasurer to Lan-fang. Call our senior scribe, Ma Joong!'

Sergeant Hoong looked doubtful. Tugging at his thin goatee, he said, 'By the same reasoning, sir, the thief might have learned the secret in any place along the road from the capital. Or even before the Treasurer left, in the capital itself!'

'No, Hoong, there's definite proof that it must have been in Tong-kang that the secret leaked out. The Treasurer says in his official statement recorded here that the side of the gold-box got cracked just before he reached Tong-kang. Presumably because of the excessive weight of the gold.'

Ma Joong brought a lean, elderly man in. The scribe bowed and wished the judge a good morning. Then he waited respectfully for the judge to address him.

'I am gathering data on the theft of the Treasurer's gold,' Judge Dee told him. 'I want you to make a trip to Tong-kang, his last halting-place before he reached Lan-fang. You'll report to the local tribunal, and try to find there someone who remembers the Treasurer's visit. I want to know whether the Treasurer received any visitors on the night he stayed there, whether a local woman companion was provided for him, whether he received any messages; in short, everything.' He selected an official blank from among the papers on his desk and jotted

10

down a few lines of introduction addressed to his colleague in Tong-kang. When he had stamped the document with the large red seal of the tribunal, he handed it to the scribe. 'You'll leave at once. While the grooms are preparing your horse, read this dossier. Try to be back here the day after tomorrow.'

'Very good, Your Honour.'

The scribe was about to make his bow when Ma Joong asked him, 'Do you know where our headman is?'

'He has gone out to arrest a vagrant, sir. There was a violent quarrel in a winehouse down town last night, and the vagrant killed a professional bully.'

'Well,' Judge Dee said, 'since that is evidently an ordinary crime of violence of the underworld, it won't necessitate much paperwork. So, get on your way! Good luck!'

When the senior scribe had left, Ma Joong said sourly, 'So that's what our good headman is doing! Arresting a murderer. And without having taken out a warrant, too! If the fellow doesn't take care of himself, he'll fall ill from working overtime, one of these days!'

'Pity we couldn't keep old Fang as headman,' the sergeant remarked. 'By the way, what is that small box there, Your Honour? I've never seen it on your desk before.'

'A box?' Judge Dee asked, roused from his thoughts. 'Oh that! I bought it at the curio-dealer's, on the corner behind the Temple of Confucius. Saw it there half an hour ago, when I was taking my morning walk. I bought it as a small birthday present for my First Lady. I'll give it to her at our festive dinner tonight.'

He picked the box up and showed it to his lieutenants.

'The character for "long life" on the cover makes it most suitable for a birthday present. The jade disc has

11

been beautifully carved into the shape of the character's antique form.' He pointed over his shoulder. 'Exactly the same style as the character used as decoration in the latticework of the window here.'

He gave the box to Ma Joong, who looked at it appraisingly and remarked, 'Just the right size for keeping visiting-cards in.' Then he brought the box closer to his eyes. 'Pity there are a few scratches on the cover. Some fool tried to scribble the word "entrance" here on one side of the disc. And on the opposite side he tried to write something like "below". Let me have it this morning, sir. After the session I'll take it to a cabinet worker I know near the south gate. He'll polish the cover nicely.'

'Yes, that's a good idea. What are you looking at?'

Ma Joong had casually opened the box. Now he was scrutinizing the inside of the cover.

'There's a small scrap of paper stuck on here,' he muttered.

'That'll be the price-tag,' the judge said. 'Peel it off, will you?'

His lieutenant put his thumbnail under a corner of the paper. Suddenly he looked up.

'No, this isn't a price-tag, sir. I see two lines in reversed writing, and in red ink. Good, it comes off. Now we can turn it over. Clumsily written. I can't make out what it says.'

He handed the tiny scrap to the judge, who raised his tufted eyebrows and read aloud:

'*I am dying of hunger and thirst. Please come and get me out. Jade. The twelfth day of the ninth month, the year of the Snake.*'

The judge looked up, annoyed. 'Why paste such a silly thing on the cover of this box?'

JUDGE DEE SHOWS A BIRTHDAY PRESENT

'Perhaps it is no joke, sir!' Ma Joong said excitedly. 'A girl called Jade, that must be a nice wench! She was kidnapped, of course!'

Sergeant Hoong smiled indulgently. He was well acquainted with Ma Joong's amorous disposition. He said quietly, 'You are always ready to rush to the rescue of damsels in distress, Brother Ma. But this is evidently only a scrap torn from the page of a romantic novel, or a play.'

'Nonsense!' Ma Joong said peevishly. 'The poor wench wrote it with her own blood, then put it in this box and threw it out of the window of the room she was kept captive in. The writing was still wet, and when the box rolled over after it hit the ground, the scrap got stuck to the cover. It happened nearly a year ago, but that's no reason why we should let the scoundrels who let her starve to death get away with it!' Turning to the judge, he asked eagerly, 'What do you think, sir?'

Judge Dee had smoothed the scrap out on his desk and was examining it, tugging at his sidewhiskers. He looked up.

'Your reasoning is quite clever, Ma Joong. However, I agree with the sergeant. If this were a genuine message of distress, then . . .' He turned his eyes to the door. 'Come in!'

The headman entered and saluted smartly. A pleased grin creased his coarse face, surrounded by a stubbly chinbeard.

'I beg to report that I have just arrested a murderer, Your Honour. A vagabond called Ah-liu. He killed a local bully last night after a quarrel in—'

'Yes, the scribe told me already. Good work, headman! I shall hear the case presently, during the morning session. Were there witnesses?'

14

'Plenty, sir! The innkeeper, two gamblers, and—'

'Good. See that they are present in court.'

After the headman had left, Judge Dee rose. He picked up the ebony box and regarded it pensively, weighing it on the palm of his hand. Then he put it in his sleeve. 'We shall pursue the matter of the queer message in this box a bit farther,' he told his two lieutenants. 'We have an hour or so left before the session begins. No matter what the message is, it has spoilt the auspicious atmosphere that must surround a birthday present. So I shall go back to the curio-dealer anyway, to select another present. I shall then ask him when and how he came by that box. You go to the chancery, Sergeant. Verify in the files on missing persons whether in the ninth month of the year of the Snake a woman called Jade was reported as having disappeared. You, Ma Joong, shall accompany me to the curio-shop. It's only a short distance; we'll walk.'

III

When Judge Dee and Ma Joong descended the broad steps at the tribunal's main gate, they saw that the main thoroughfare leading to the southern city gate was quite crowded already, notwithstanding the early hour and the muggy heat. The slender spire of the pagoda in the Lotus Lake was only vaguely visible through the humid haze that hung over the city.

The judge walked ahead. Nobody recognized him as the magistrate, for he was still wearing his simple blue robe, and had exchanged his high official headdress of black gauze for a small skull-cap. Ma Joong, who was following close behind him, wore the uniform of an officer of the tribunal: a brown robe with black belt and borders, and a flat black cap.

After they had gone some way, Ma Joong suddenly halted in his steps. A few paces away a pair of large, burning eyes were fixing him with an intense, unwavering stare. He got a brief glimpse of a pale, handsome face, partly concealed by the piece of cloth the woman wore over her head, Tartar fashion. She seemed unusually tall. Just as he was going to ask what she wanted, two coolies carrying a large wooden box on their shoulders came between them. When they had passed, the woman had become lost in the crowd.

16

Judge Dee turned round to him and pointed at the high roof of the Temple of Confucius ahead. 'The shop is on the corner of the second side-street behind the temple, on the right.' Then, seeing Ma Joong's bewildered face, he asked, 'What is wrong with you?'

'I just saw a most extraordinary woman, sir. She had uncommonly large eyes, and—'

'I wish you wouldn't always stare at every female person you meet!' the judge told him peevishly. 'Come along, we haven't much time!'

In the narrow side-street behind the temple less people were about. An agreeable coolness greeted them when they had gone inside the small, semi-dark curio-shop. An old man with an untidy long beard came hurriedly up to the counter when he recognized the judge.

'Is there anything else I can do for Your Excellency?' he croaked with a toothless smile.

'When I came here this morning,' Judge Dee replied, 'I forgot that I also wanted a nice piece of jade. A pair of bracelets, or a long hairpin, perhaps.'

The dealer took a square tray from under the counter.

'Here Your Excellency will find a choice collection.'

The judge rummaged among the pieces of jewelry. He selected a pair of antique bracelets of white jade, carved into the shape of plumblossom sprigs. Putting them aside, he inquired the price.

'One silver piece. A special price for a special customer!'

'I'll take them. By the way, could you tell me perhaps where you got the ebony box I bought? I always like to know the provenance of the antiques I buy, you see.'

The old man pushed his skull-cap back and scratched his grey head.

17

'Where did I get it now? Allow me to look it up in my register, noble lord! One moment, please!'

'Why didn't you beat the price down, sir?' Ma Joong asked, indignant. 'One whole silver piece! One wonders how the old rascal keeps alive!'

'The bracelets are worth it. And I am sure my First Lady will like them.'

The curio-dealer emerged from the back of the shop. He placed a dog-eared volume on the counter. Pointing with a spidery forefinger at an entry, he mumbled:

'Yes, here I have it! I bought the box four months ago, from Mr Lee Ko.'

'Who is that?' the judge asked curtly.

'Well, Lee Ko is what you might call a minor painter, Excellency. He specializes in landscapes. Paints landscapes all day, more of them than people care to buy! Who wants to buy new landscapes, I ask you, my lord? Pictures of mountains that you can see gratis everyday, right outside our city! If it was antique pictures now, then . . .'

'Where does Mr Lee live?'

'Not far from here, Excellency. In the street next to the Bell Tower. An old, rambling house, sir! Yes, now I remember! The box was in a basket of old junk Mr Lee wanted to dispose of. All covered with mud, it was. If Mr Lee had seen that fine piece of green jade on the cover . . .' His toothless mouth broadened in a sly grin. But then he added quickly: 'I paid a fair price for the lot, Excellency! Mr Lee's brother owns a gold- and silver-shop, not too big, but . . . I want to stay on the right side of the Lee family, sir. I might do business with Mr Lee Mai, some day . . .'

'If Lee Ko has a well-to-do elder brother, why then is he living in poverty?' Judge Dee asked.

18

The other shrugged his thin shoulders.

'They had a quarrel last year, people say. Your Excellency knows how it is nowadays, the people don't understand any more that fathers and sons, elder and younger brothers should always keep together. I always say—'

'Quite. Here is the money. No, you needn't wrap them up.'

The judge put the jade bracelets in his sleeve. When they were outside he said to Ma Joong, 'It's only a ten minutes' walk to the Bell Tower. Since we have pursued our inquiries this far, we had better call on Mr Lee Ko.'

They crossed the main thoroughfare again and walked round the raised platform of the Bell Tower. The bronze surface of the huge bell suspended from the red-lacquered rafters shone dully. It was beaten every morning, to rouse the citizens at daybreak. An obliging water carrier directed them to a barrack-like wooden house in a narrow back street, apparently inhabited by small shopkeepers.

The front door was of plain boards, the cracks here and there clumsily repaired. The windows flanking the door were shuttered.

'Lee's house doesn't look very prosperous,' Judge Dee commented as he rapped his knuckles on the door.

'He should've become a curio-dealer!' said Ma Joong sourly.

They heard the sound of heavy footsteps. A crossbar was removed and the door swung open.

The tall, slovenly dressed man suddenly stepped back. 'Who . . . what . . . ?' he stammered. Evidently he had been expecting only a tradesman. Judge Dee quietly took in the other's lean face with its small black moustache and large, alert eyes. His long brown gown, stained with paint, hung loosely about him; his black velvet cap was threadbare.

19

'Are you Mr Lee Ko, the painter?' Judge Dee asked politely. And when the other nodded silently, he went on, 'I am magistrate Dee, and this is my assistant, Ma Joong.' Noticing that Lee's face grew pale, he resumed affably, 'This is quite an informal visit, Mr Lee! I am interested in landscape painting, you see, and I have heard that you are an expert. When my morning walk took me to this neighbourhood, I decided on the spur of the moment to drop in and have a look at your work.'

'A great honour, sir! A great honour indeed!' Lee said quickly. Then his face fell. 'Unfortunately, my house is in a terrible state just now. My assistant didn't come home last night. He always cleans up for me, you see. If Your Excellency could come perhaps after . . .'

'I don't mind a bit!' the judge interrupted him jovially and stepped inside the dark hall.

The painter took them to a large, low-ceilinged room at the back, dimly lit by two broad windows pasted over with soiled tissue-paper. He pushed a ramshackle high-backed chair up to the table on trestles in the centre, and offered Ma Joong a bamboo tabouret.

When Lee went to the wall table to prepare tea, Judge Dee glanced casually at the litter of rolls of paper and silk and vases of paint brushes on the table. The paint in the small platters had dried to a cracked crust, and a thin film of dust covered the inkslab. The painter had apparently just taken his breakfast, for on the end of the table stood a cracked bowl of rice gruel, and beside it lay a piece of oil-paper with a small quantity of pickles on it.

Against the wall on the left hung dozens of landscape paintings, all done in black and white. Some of them the judge thought quite impressive. When he turned to gaze at the scrolls displayed on the wall opposite, however, he frowned. All those pictures represented Buddhist deities. Not the serene, beautiful gods and goddesses of older Buddhism, but the half-naked, fierce-looking demons of the later esoteric school. Terrifying figures with many heads and arms, monstrous faces, rolling eyes and wide-open mouths, wearing garlands of severed human heads. Some were clasping their female counterparts in their arms. These pictures were executed in full colours, with a liberal use of gold and green.

When Lee had put two teacups on the table, the judge remarked, 'I like your landscapes, Mr Lee. They aim at achieving the grand manner of our ancient masters.'

The painter looked pleased.

'I love landscapes, sir. In spring and autumn I make long trips in the mountains to the north and east of our city. I don't think there's one peak in this district which I haven't climbed! In my paintings I try to render the essence of the scenes of nature I have seen.'

Judge Dee nodded with approval. He turned round and pointed at the religious paintings.

'Why should a high-minded artist like you stoop to those barbarian horrors?'

Lee sat down on a bamboo bench in front of the window. Smiling thinly, he replied, 'Landscapes don't keep my rice-bowl full, sir! But there's a big demand for those Buddhist scrolls among the Tartar and Uigur population of this city. As you know, these people believe in that disgusting new creed that teaches that the intercourse of man and woman is a replica of the mating of Heaven and Earth and a means of reaching salvation. The devotees identify themselves with those fierce gods and their female counterparts. Their ritual includes—'

Judge Dee raised his hand.

'I know all about those abominable excesses, committed under the cloak of religion. They lead to lechery and dark crimes. When I was serving as magistrate of Han-yuan I had to deal with several disgusting murders committed in a Taoist monastery where that ritual was secretly followed.* Whether the Buddhists took this ritual over from the Taoists or vice versa, I don't know and I care less.' He angrily tugged at his beard. Then he gave the painter a sharp look. 'You don't mean to say that those awful rites are still being practised here in this district?'

'Oh no, sir. Not any more. Eight or ten years ago, however, the Temple of the Purple Clouds, on the hill just outside the east city gate, belonged to that sect, and many Tartar and other barbarian Buddhists from over the border went to worship there. But then the authorities stepped in and the monks and nuns had to leave. The Buddhists of this city, however, still cling to that faith. They buy these pictures to hang above their house altars. They firmly believe that those fierce gods protect them against all evil and ensure long life and many sons.'

'Silly superstitions!' the judge said with disdain. 'The original teaching of the Buddha contains many a lofty thought. I myself, being an orthodox Confucianist—as you are too, I trust, Mr Lee—don't hold with Buddhist idolatry in any form. I would like to order a landscape from you. I have long wanted to have in my library a painting of the border region, suggesting the contrast between the mountains and the wide, open plain, and I would be very pleased if you would do that for me. I shall also gladly recommend you to my acquaintances. On condition, however, that you stop doing those repulsive Buddhist pictures!'

'I gladly obey your orders, sir!'

'Good!' Judge Dee took the ebony box from his sleeve.

* See The Haunted Monastery, London 1963.

22

Putting it on the table, he asked, 'Did this box formerly belong to your collection?'

He watched the painter's face eagerly but Lee only showed blank astonishment.

'No, never saw it before, sir. There are dozens of them in the market, of course. The local cabinet workers make them from left-over pieces of ebony, and people buy them for keeping their seals or visiting-cards in. But I have never seen such a nice antique specimen. And if I had seen it, I wouldn't have been able to buy it!'

Judge Dee put the box back into his sleeve. 'Does your brother never buy pictures from you?' he asked casually.

Lee's face fell. He replied curtly, 'My brother is a businessman. He has no interest in art and despises all artists.'

'Do you live here all alone with your assistant?'

'Yes sir. I hate the bother of keeping a regular household. Yang—that's the name of my man—is a capable fellow. He's a student of literature who couldn't take part in the final examination because of lack of funds. He does the house and he also helps me prepare paint and so on. Pity you can't meet him.' Seeing that the judge was rising, he resumed quickly, 'May I pour you another cup of tea, sir? It isn't often that I have the advantage of conversing with such a famous scholar and—'

'I am sorry, Mr Lee, but I have to return to the tribunal now. Thank you for the tea. And don't forget about that painting of the border scene!'

Lee respectfully conducted them to the door.

'That slick artist is a damned liar, sir!' Ma Joong burst out when they were walking down the street. 'The old geezer in the curio-shop was sure he had bought the box from Lee. And he doesn't make any mistakes about his business. Not he!'

'At first,' Judge Dee said slowly, 'Lee impressed me rather favourably. Later, however, I wasn't so sure.' He halted. 'While I am going on to the tribunal, you might as well ask in a shop or so around here what they think of Lee. And also ask about that assistant of his. Just to round out the picture, so to speak.'

Ma Joong nodded.

He saw only one prominent shop-sign in the narrow alley. It proclaimed in large letters that there gauze fine as gossamer was cut accurately to measure. The tailor was rolling up a bolt of silk. In the rear of the shop four elderly women were gathered round a long, narrow table, busy stitching and embroidering. The tailor greeted Ma Joong civilly enough. But his face fell when he asked whether he knew the painter.

'As poor as a starving rat!' he said disgustedly. 'I see him pass by here occasionally, but he has never yet bought a stitch of clothing! And that assistant of his, he's just a tramp. Keeps irregular hours, and associates with all kinds of hoodlums. He often rouses this decent, quiet neighbourhood when he comes home singing and shouting, as drunk as a lord!'

'Young men of letters like a gay night, now and then,' Ma Joong said soothingly.

'Young man of letters, my foot! Yang is just a vagabond! Still likes to doll himself up, though. He has bought a new robe from me, worse luck! Hasn't paid me one copper! I would've raised a row about that, but . . .' He leaned over the counter and looked the street up and down. 'I have to be careful, you see. Wouldn't like him to come here with his hoodlums some day and throw garbage buckets over my fine stock of silk. . . .'

'If Yang is such a good-for-nothing, why does Mr Lee keep him in his service?'

24

'Because Mr Lee isn't one jot better than him! Birds of a feather, that's what those two are, sir! And why doesn't Mr Lee marry, I ask you? It's true he's poor, but no matter how poor a man is, he can always find a girl who is poorer still, so that he can establish a regular household, as every decent man should. The two of them are all alone in that rambling shack, sir; they don't even have a char-woman come in. Heaven only knows what goes on there of nights!'

The tailor gave Ma Joong an expectant look, but when the tall man didn't ask for details, the tailor bent his head close and resumed in a low voice, 'I am not a one to tell tales, mind you. Live and let live, I always say. Therefore I'll say only this: some time ago my neighbour saw a woman slip inside there; at midnight it was, he said. And when I told that to our grocer, he remembered having seen Lee let a woman out, at dawn, if you please! Such goings-on give a neighbourhood a bad name, sir. And that affects my custom.'

Ma Joong remarked that it was a sad world. After he had learned that the student's full name was Yang Mou-te, he said goodbye. He strolled back to the tribunal, cursing the heat.

IV

When Ma Joong entered Judge Dee's private office, Sergeant Hoong was assisting the judge into his heavy official robe of green brocade with the gold-embroidered collar. While the judge was adjusting his winged black cap in front of the cap-mirror, Ma Joong reported on his conversation with the tailor.

'I don't know what to think about all this,' Judge Dee said. 'Hoong has gone over the file on missing persons but he also drew a blank. Tell Ma Joong what you found, Sergeant!'

Sergeant Hoong picked up a sheet of notepaper from the desk.

'On the fourth day of the ninth month,' he told Ma Joong, 'two persons were reported missing. A Tartar horse-dealer here said his daughter had suddenly disappeared; but she turned up the following month, complete with a husband from over the border and a small baby. Second, the brother of a metal-worker and locksmith called Ming Ao reported that he went out on the sixth of the ninth month and never came back. To be quite sure, I went over all the entries belonging to the year of the Snake, but no person of the name Jade was mentioned.'

The booming sound of the large bronze gong at the

entrance of the tribunal came towards them. It was beaten three times, indicating that the session of the tribunal was about to begin.

Sergeant Hoong drew the curtain that separated Judge Dee's office from the court room aside. The violet curtain was embroidered in gold thread with a large image of the unicorn, the traditional symbol of perspicacity. The judge ascended the dais and sat down behind the high bench, covered with a piece of red cloth, the front side of which hung down to the floor. On the bench lay a small pile of official documents, beside it a large, rectangular package wrapped up in oil-paper. The judge bestowed a curious glance upon the package, then he folded his arms in his wide sleeves and inspected the court.

It was fairly cool in the spacious, high-ceilinged hall. There were only a dozen or so spectators. They loitered at the back. Evidently they had come to escape the heat outside rather than to assist at an exciting murder trial. Eight constables stood at attention in two rows of four in front of the dais, their headman somewhat apart, his heavy whip in his hand. Two pairs of iron handcuffs dangled from his broad leather belt. Behind him the judge saw four men of the labouring class, dressed in neat blue jackets and looking ill at ease. To the left of the dais two clerks were sitting at a low table, their writing-brushes held ready for recording the court proceedings.

After the sergeant and Ma Joong had stood themselves behind Judge Dee's armchair, the judge took the gavel, an oblong piece of hardwood, and rapped it on the bench.

'I declare the session of the tribunal of Lan-fang open!' he announced. He called the roll, then ordered the headman to have the accused led before the bench.

On a sign from the headman two constables went to the door-opening on the left and dragged a beanpole of a man before the dais. He was dressed in a patched brown jacket and wide trousers. Judge Dee quickly took in his long, sun-tanned face adorned by a ragged moustache and a short chinbeard; the long, unkempt hair hung over his forehead in greasy locks. Then the constables pressed him down on his knees on the stone flags in front of the bench. The headman stood himself close by the kneeling man, swinging his whip to and fro.

Judge Dee consulted the paper on top of the pile before him. Looking up, he asked sternly, 'Are you Ah-liu, aged thirty-two, of no fixed profession or domicile?'

'Yes I am,' the accused wailed. 'But I want to say here and now that—'

The headman let the butt-end of his whip descend on Ah-liu's shoulders. 'Only answer His Excellency's questions!' he barked at the prisoner.

'State the Court's case against the prisoner, headman!'

The headman stood at attention, cleared his throat importantly and began:

'Last night this man ate the evening-rice in Chow's tavern, just inside the east city gate, together with Seng-san, a notorious bully of that neighbourhood. They had four jugs of wine and quarrelled over the payment. The innkeeper Chow intervened, and a compromise was reached. Thereupon Ah-liu and Seng-san began to throw dice. After the latter had been losing heavily for some time, he suddenly jumped up and accused Ah-liu of cheating. A hand-to-hand fight resulted, Ah-liu trying to bash in Seng-san's head with an empty wine-jug. The innkeeper enlisted the help of the other guests. Together they succeeded in persuading the two to leave the premises. Seng-san was heard to tell Ah-liu that he would settle his hash in the deserted temple. That means the old Buddhist Temple of the Purple Clouds, Your Honour, on the hill outside the east gate. It has been standing empty for more than ten years now, and all kinds of riff-raff pass the night there.'

'Did the accused and Seng-san actually proceed there together?' Judge Dee asked.

'Indeed they did, Your Honour. The guards at the east gate stated that the two passed through the gate one hour before midnight, violently abusing each other all the time. The guards warned them that they were about to close the gate for the night, and Ah-liu shouted that he would never come back anyway.'

Ah-liu raised his head to say something. But as the headman raised his whip he quickly bent his head again to the floor.

'This morning, just after dawn, the hunter Meng came to the tribunal and reported that when entering the main hall of the temple to take a rest there, he found a dead body lying in front of the altar. I at once set out there with two of my men. The head had been severed from the neck and was lying beside the body, in a pool of blood. I identified the victim as the bully Seng-san. The murder weapon was lying there too, namely a heavy double axe, of Tartar make. I instituted a search of the temple grounds and found the accused lying asleep under a tree, at the edge of the temple garden. His jacket was stained with blood. Since I feared that he might escape if I went to take out a warrant first, I arrested him then and there on the technical charge of vagrancy. When he told me that the last place he had visited in town was Chow's tavern, I proceeded there at once and Chow told me about the quarrel. Mr Chow is present here in court to deliver testimony, together with two of his customers who witnessed the quarrel, and the hunter Meng.'

Judge Dee nodded. He turned round to Ma Joong and

asked in a low voice, 'Isn't it rather unusual that a quarrel between ruffians is settled with an axe?'

'Indeed, sir,' Ma Joong replied. 'One expects a knife thrust, or a blow on the head with a heavy club.'

'Let's see the murder weapon!'

Ma Joong undid the oil-paper. They saw a double axe with a crooked handle about three feet long. The razor-sharp edges were covered with dried blood. The bronze butt end was wrought into the shape of a grinning devil's head.

'How did the murderer obtain this outlandish weapon, headman?'

'He found it ready to hand, Your Honour. The temple hall is empty except for the old altar table against the back wall. But in a niche in the side wall stand two halberds and two axes. When the temple was still inhabited, those weapons were used during the ritual dances. They were left behind when the priests vacated the temple. No one has dared to steal them, because they are sacred objects that bring bad luck.'

'Did Seng-san have any relatives here, headman?'

'No sir. He had a brother called Lao-woo, but that fellow moved to the neighbour district Tong-kang some time ago.'

Sergeant Hoong bent over to the judge and said, 'I saw in the copies of official proceedings forwarded by Your Honour's colleague there that he condemned Lao-woo to six months in jail recently, together with the woman he was living with. The charge was the stealing of a pig.'

'I see.' Then the judge said, 'Ah-liu, report to this court exactly what happened last night!'

'Nothing, noble lord, nothing at all. I swear it! Seng-san is my best friend, why should I want to . . . ?'

'You had a violent quarrel with him and you tried to

30

bash in his head,' Judge Dee cut him short. 'Do you deny that too?'

'Of course not, sir! Seng-san and me, we are always quarrelling, it helps to pass the time. Later Seng-san said I was cheating at dice, and I was. I always do, and Seng-san is always trying to catch me at it. That's part of the fun! Believe me, noble lord, I didn't murder him. I swear it! I have never so much as harmed a hair on nobody's head, I would never—'

The judge rapped his gavel.

'State what happened after you two had left the tavern!'

'We walked together to the east gate, noble lord, cursing each other in a friendly manner. When we had passed the gate, we walked on arm in arm, singing a song. Seng-san helped me to get up the steps, for I was very tired. I'd been carrying wood the whole afternoon for that skinflint of a . . . Well, when we are up in the yard of the temple, Seng-san says, "I'll walk on to the hall, I'll sleep on the altar table!" I feel so sleepy that I lay myself down under a tree then and there. I woke up only this morning so find that son of a . . .' He checked himself as the headman raised his whip again and concluded sullenly, '. . . to find the officer here was kicking my ribs and shouting that I was a murderer!'

'Was there anybody else about in the deserted temple?'

'Not a living soul, noble lord!'

'Has the coroner examined the remains, headman?'

'Yes, Your Honour. Here is his report.'

The headman took a folded sheet of paper from his sleeve and placed it on the bench, respectfully, with both hands. Judge Dee glanced through the document, Ma Joong and the sergeant reading it over his shoulder.

'Funny that he went to the trouble of severing the

31

head!' muttered Ma Joong. 'Cutting his throat would've done the job!'

Judge Dee looked round at him.

'The coroner states,' he said in a low voice, 'that the body did not show any scars or other signs of violence. Since Seng-san was a professional bully, that also seems a little curious to me.' He thought for a few moments, smoothing his long black beard. Then he went on to his two lieutenants: 'Our coroner is a pharmacist by profession. A good man, but he has little experience of forensic medicine. I think we'd better have a look at the remains ourselves before we go on with the interrogation.' He rapped his gavel and spoke:

'Lead the accused back to jail, headman! There will be a recess until further notice.'

He rose and disappeared behind the unicorn screen, followed by Sergeant Hoong and Ma Joong.

V

The three men walked through the chancery to the jail in the back of the compound, where a side hall served as mortuary.

There was a musty smell in the narrow hall. In the centre of the red-tiled floor stood a high trestle table. On it lay a long shape, covered by a reed-mat, and on the floor beside it was a large, round basket.

Judge Dee pointed at the basket. 'Let's first see the head,' he told Ma Joong.

His lieutenant placed the basket on the table. When he had raised the lid he made a face.

'Messy affair, sir!' Having pulled his neckcloth up over his mouth and nose, he lifted the head from the basket by the long hair, clotted with blood. He laid it face up beside the basket.

The judge observed the grisly exhibit in silence, his hands behind his back. Seng-san had a bloated, sun-burnt face, the left cheek disfigured by an ugly old scar. The broken, bloodshot eyes were partly concealed by the matted locks of hair stuck to the low, wrinkled forehead. A ragged moustache hung over the sensual mouth, its thick lips distorted to a sneer that showed the brown, uneven teeth. The stump of the neck was a mass of torn skin and coagulated blood.

33

'Not a very prepossessing face,' Judge Dee remarked. 'Pull that reed-mat away, Hoong!'

The naked, headless body was well-proportioned, the hips slender, the shoulders broad. The arms were long and showed heavy muscles.

'Fairly tall, powerful chap,' Ma Joong commented. 'Hardly the type that meekly tenders his neck to have his head cut off.' He bent over the body and studied the stump of the neck. 'Aha, here we have a blue weal, and abrasions. Seng-san was strangled, sir. With a thin cord, and probably from behind.'

Judge Dee nodded.

'You must be right, Ma Joong, that weal is clear proof. One would have expected the face to look different, but the subsequent severing of the head accounts for that. Now, when would this foul crime have been committed?' The judge felt the arms and the legs, then bent the right elbow. 'Judging by the condition of the corpse, death must have occurred about midnight. That is at least one fact that accords with our headman's theory.' He was about to let the arm of the dead man go when he suddenly checked himself. He opened the balled fist and examined the smooth palm, then he scrutinized the fingers. He let the arm drop and walked to the other end of the table to have a look at the feet.

Righting himself, he said to Sergeant Hoong, 'That blood-spattered bundle in the corner there contains the deceased's clothes, I suppose? Put it here on the table and open it!'

The judge selected from the pile of clothes a pair of patched trousers, and laid them over the legs of the dead body. 'Just as I thought!' he muttered.

Giving his two assistants a sombre look, he said:

'I was very wrong, my friends, when this morning I

34

said that this was just another crime of violence of the underworld. To begin with, it was a double murder.'

They stared at him in incomprehension.

'A double murder?' Sergeant Hoong exclaimed. 'What does that mean, sir?'

'It means that not one but two people were murdered. The heads were severed so that the bodies could be switched. Can't you see that this isn't Seng-san's body? Compare the sun-burnt face with the smooth white skin of the hands and forearms of the body, and look at these well-kept hands, at the feet without callouses! Moreover, this is the body of a fairly tall man, though Seng-san's trousers are too long for him. Our headman has still a lot to learn!'

'I'll call the stupid ass at once!' Ma Joong muttered. 'Then we'll give him a sound . . .'

'No, you'll do nothing of the sort!' Judge Dee said quickly. 'The murderer must have had a very strong reason for making it appear that only Seng-san was murdered, and that this is Seng-san's body. We shan't undeceive him. For the time being, that is.'

'Where's Seng-san's body, and the head of that unknown party?' Ma Joong asked, perplexed.

'That's what I want to know too,' the judge replied curtly. 'Heavens, a double murder, and we haven't even the faintest inkling of the motive of this callous crime!' He tugged at his moustache, staring down at Seng-san's distorted face. Then he turned round and said curtly, 'We'll go to the jail next door and have a talk with Ahliu.'

The small cell was so dark that they could hardly make out the huddled shape of the prisoner who was sitting on the other side of the iron bars. When he saw the three men stepping up to the door, he hastily scrambled away

35

to the farthest corner with a loud clanking of chains.

'Don't beat me!' he shouted frantically. 'I swear that I . . .'

'Shut up!' the judge barked, then continued in a more friendly voice: 'I just came to have a talk with you about your friend Seng-san. If it wasn't you who murdered him up there in the deserted temple, who did? And how did you get the blood on your jacket?'

Ah-liu crawled to the door. Hugging his knees with his manacled hands, he began in a whining voice, 'I wouldn't know, noble lord. How could I? Seng-san had a few enemies, of course. Who hasn't, with all the competition that's going on nowadays? But none that would risk his life to kill him. No sir. As to the blood, only Heaven knows how it got on my clothes. It wasn't there when I left the tavern, that I know!' He shook his head and began again. 'Seng-san was a tough fellow, he knew how to use his hands. A knife too, for that matter. Holy heaven, suppose it was . . .' Suddenly he broke off.

'Speak up, rascal! Suppose it was who?'

'Well . . . I think it must have been the ghost, sir. The phantom of the temple, as we call her. A woman all dressed up in a long shroud, sir. She walks in the old garden there, when there's a full moon. A horrible vampire, sir. Likes to gnaw off a man's head. We never go there when—'

'Stop talking nonsense!' the judge interrupted him impatiently. 'Did Seng-san have a quarrel with someone recently? A real quarrel, I mean, not just a drunken brawl?'

'Well, he had a mighty big row with his brother, sir; a couple of weeks ago, it was. Lao-woo, that's what his brother is called. Not quite as tall as Seng-san, but a mean bastard all right. He took Seng-san's wench, and

36

Seng-san swore he'd kill him for that. Then Lao-woo left for Tong-kang. With the skirt. But a woman, that's no reason for killing a man, is it, sir? If it had been money now . . .'

'Did Seng-san have among his friends or acquaintances a fairly tall, lean chap? Kind of dandy, say a shop clerk or something like that?'

Ah-liu thought hard, wrinkling his low brow. Then he replied, 'Well, yes, I did see him a few times with a tallish fellow who was rather neatly dressed in a blue gown. Had a real cap on his head too. I asked Seng-san who he was and what they were talking about so busily, but he just told me to shut up and mind my own business. Which I did.'

'Would you recognize that man again if you saw him?'

'No sir. They met after dark, in the front yard of the temple. He had no beard, I think. Only a moustache.'

'All right, Ah-liu. I hope you told all you know. For your own sake!'

While they were walking back to the office, Judge Dee told his two lieutenants, 'Ah-liu's remarks bear the hall-mark of truth. But somebody went out of his way to make Ah-liu the scapegoat. He is safer in jail, for the time being. Tell the headman that the session is adjourned till tomorrow, Sergeant. I must change now, for I promised my ladies I would take the noon-rice with them, on this festive day. Afterwards, Hoong, I shall go with you and the headman to the deserted temple, to view the scene of the double murder. As for you, Ma Joong, I want you to go this afternoon to the north-west quarter where the Tartars, Uigurs and other barbarians live. Since the murderer used a Tartar axe, he may well have been a Tartar, or a Chinese citizen who associates with those foreigners. You have to be very familiar with

37

those axes with crooked handles to use them as effectively as the murderer did. Just go round the low-class eating-houses where the rabble hangs out, and make discreet inquiries!'

'I can do better than that, sir!' Ma Joong said eagerly. 'I shall ask Tulbee!'

Sergeant Hoong gave the judge a meaningful look but tactfully refrained from comment. Tulbee was an Uigur prostitute whom Ma Joong had violently fallen in love with six months before.* It had been a brief affair, for he had soon tired of her rather overwhelming charms, while she proved to have an incurable fondness for rancid butter-tea and an equally incurable aversion to washing herself properly. When he had, moreover, discovered that she had a steady lover already, a Mongolian camel driver whom she had given two boys of four and seven, he ended the relationship in an elegant manner. He used his savings for buying her out, and established her in an open-air soup kitchen of her own. The camel driver married her, Ma Joong acting as best man at a wedding feast of roast lamb and Mongolian raw liquor that lasted till dawn and gave him the worst hangover he had had for years.

After a brief pause, Judge Dee said cautiously, 'As a rule those people are very reticent concerning the affairs of their own race. However, since you know the girl well, she might talk more freely to you. Anyway, it's worth a try-out. Come and report to me when you are back.'

Sergeant Hoong and Ma Joong ate their noon-rice together, in the guardroom. Ma Joong had ordered a soldier to bring a large jug of wine from the nearest tavern.

'I know the rotgut the old girl serves up,' he said

* See *The Chinese Maze Murders*, London 1962.

38

wryly as he put his cup down. 'Therefore I have to line my stomach beforehand, you see! Now I'd better change into old clothes, so as not to be too conspicuous. Good luck with the search in the temple!'

After Ma Joong had left, Sergeant Hoong finished his tea and strolled over to Judge Dee's private residence at the back of the tribunal compound. The old housemaster informed him that, after the noon-rice, the judge had gone to the back garden, together with his three ladies. The sergeant nodded and walked on. He was the only male member of the personnel of the tribunal allowed to enter Judge Dee's women's quarters, and he was very proud of that privilege.

It was fairly cool in the garden, for it had been laid out expertly by a previous magistrate whose hobby was landscape gardening. High oak and acacia trees spread their branches over the winding footpath that was paved with smooth black stones of irregular shape. At every turn one heard the murmur of the brook that meandered through the undergrowth, here and there broken by clusters of flowering shrubs of carefully matched colours.

The last turn brought the sergeant to a small clearing, bordered by mossy rocks. The Second and Third Ladies, sitting on a rustic stone bench under high, rustling bamboos, were gazing at the lotus pond farther down, on the garden's lowest level. Beyond was the outer wall, camouflaged by cleverly spaced pine trees. In the centre of the lotus pond stood a small water-pavilion, its pointed roof with the gracefully upturned eaves supported by six slender, red-lacquered pillars. Judge Dee and his First Lady were inside, bent over the table by the balustrade.

'The judge is going to write,' the Second Lady informed Hoong. 'We stayed behind here so as not to disturb him.' She had a pleasant homely face; her hair was done up in

39

a simple coil at the back of her head; and she wore a jacket of violet silk over a white robe. It was her task to supervise the household accounts. The Third Lady, slender in her long-sleeved gown of blue silk, gathered under the bosom by a red sash, wore her hair in an elaborate high chignon which set off to advantage her sensitive, finely chiselled face. Her main interests were painting and calligraphy, while she was also fond of outdoor sports, especially horse-riding. She was in charge of the tuition of Judge Dee's children. Sergeant Hoong gave them a friendly nod and descended the stone stairs leading down to the lotus pond.

He went up the curved marble bridge that spanned the pond. The water-pavilion was built on the highest point of the curve. Judge Dee was standing in front of the table, a large writing-brush in his hand. He looked speculatively at the sheet of red paper spread out on the table top. His First Lady was busily preparing ink on the small side table. She had an oval, regular face, and her hair was done up in three heavy coils, fixed by a narrow, golden hairband. The tailored robe of blue and white embroidered silk showed her fine figure, inclining to portliness now that she was celebrating her thirty-ninth birthday. The judge had married her when she was nineteen and he twenty. She was the eldest daughter of a high official, his father's best friend. Having received an excellent classical education and being a woman of strong personality, she directed the entire household with a firm hand. Now she stopped rubbing the ink-cake on the stone, and motioned to her husband that it was ready. Judge Dee moistened the brush, pushed his right sleeve back from his wrist, then wrote the character for 'long life', nearly four feet high, in one powerful sweeping movement.

Sergeant Hoong, who had been waiting on the bridge

till the judge was ready, now stepped into the pavilion. 'Magnificent calligraphy, sir!' he exclaimed.

'I wanted that auspicious character in the master's own handwriting, Hoong!' the First Lady said with a satisfied smile. 'Tonight we shall display it on the wall of the dining-room!'

The Second and Third Ladies came rushing towards the pond to admire the writing too. They clapped their hands excitedly.

'Well,' Judge Dee said smiling, 'it couldn't but turn out well, seeing that my First Lady made the ink and you two prepared the red paper and the brush! I must be leaving now, for I have to go and have a look at the deserted temple. Some vagabonds had a scuffle there last night. If there's time, I shall call on the Abbess in the Hermitage and tell her that I am planning to post a regular guardpost on the hill.'

'Please do that!' the Second Lady said eagerly. 'The Abbess is alone in the Hermitage with only one maid-servant.'

'You ought to persuade the Abbess to move into the city,' the First Lady remarked. 'There are two or three empty shrines here where she could settle down. That would save her coming such a long way on the days she teaches us flower arrangement.'

'I'll do my best,' the judge promised. His ladies liked the Abbess, who was one of the few nice friends they had in Lan-fang. 'I may be late,' he added, 'but you'll be busy the whole afternoon anyway, receiving the wives of the notables who come to offer their congratulations. I'll try to be back as early as possible.'

His three ladies conducted him to the entrance of the garden.

VI

Judge Dee's large official palankeen was standing ready in the front yard, eight sturdy bearers by its side. The headman was also waiting there, accompanied by ten constables on horseback. Judge Dee entered the palankeen, followed by Sergeant Hoong.

While they were being carried to the east gate, the sergeant asked: 'Why should the murderer have gone to all the trouble of severing the heads of his victims, sir? And why switch the bodies?'

'The obvious answer, Sergeant, is that, although the murderer—or murderers!—didn't mind Seng-san being identified as one of the victims, for some mysterious reason he didn't want Seng-san's *body* found. At the same time he wanted to conceal the fact that there had been a second murder, and he wanted to hide the identity of his second victim. But there could be also other, less obvious reasons. However, let's not worry about that yet. Our first task is to discover Seng-san's body, and the head of the other victim. Those must be hidden somewhere in or near the deserted temple.'

When the cortège had passed through the east city gate, a few loafers hanging around the small shops and street stalls lining the country road went to follow, curious to know what was afoot. But the headman raised his whip and barked at them to stay behind.

A little further on an ornamental stone arch at the foot of the wooded mountain slope indicated the beginning of the flight of steps leading uphill. The headman and the constables dismounted. While the bearers were lowering Judge Dee's palankeen to the ground, he said to the sergeant quickly:

'Remember, Hoong, that our men are not to know exactly what we are looking for! I'll tell them it's a large box or something like that.' The judge descended and bestowed a dubious look on the steep staircase. 'A stiff climb on a hot day, headman!'

'Nearly two hundred steps, Your Honour. But it's the quickest way. Behind the temple there's a footpath that goes down the slope in an easy descent to the highway, and from there it's but a short walk to the north city gate. But then it takes you more than an hour to reach the top of the hill. Only hunters and woodgatherers use that road. The riff-raff that stay in the temple overnight go up these stairs.'

'All right.' The judge gathered up the front of his robe and began the ascent of the broad, weatherbeaten stone steps.

Half-way up the judge ordered a brief rest, for he had noticed that the sergeant was breathing heavily. Arrived on the top of the stairs, they saw a weed-overgrown clearing among tall trees. On the other side rose a triple temple gate of grey stone with, on either side, a formidable-looking high wall. Over the central arch of the gate appeared three characters in multicoloured mosaic, reading Tzu-yün-szu, 'Temple of the Purple Clouds'.

'The narrow pathway along the wall on the right leads to the small new temple, the so-called Hermitage, sir,' explained the headman. 'The Abbess lives there, with one maidservant. I haven't asked them yet whether they heard or saw anything last night.'

'I want to see the scene of the crime first,' Judge Dee told him. 'Lead the way!'

The paved front courtyard was overgrown with weeds and the walls were crumbling here and there, but the temple's main hall with its high roof, flanked by two three-storeyed towers, had withstood the ravages of time intact.

'This outlandish architecture,' the judge remarked to Sergeant Hoong, 'can of course never come near the perfection of ours. I have to admit, however, that from a technical point of view the Indian builders did a good job. Those two towers are absolutely symmetrical. I gather that this temple was built three hundred years ago, and it is still in a remarkably good state of repair. Where did you find Ah-liu, headman?'

The headman took them to the edge of the wilderness on the left of the courtyard. On the right was a piece of wasteland, strewn with large boulders. The judge noticed that it was slightly cooler here than down in the city. The warm air was filled with the incessant strident chirping of cicadas.

'This wilderness was once an extensive, well-kept garden, Your Honour,' the headman explained. 'Now it's a mass of tangled vegetation where even the scoundrels who gather in the temple and courtyard don't dare to go. It is said that there are many poisonous snakes.' Pointing to an old oak tree, he went on: 'The accused was lying under that tree, sir, his head resting on the raised root. My conjecture is that he meant to take to his heels after he had murdered Seng-san. But he stumbled in the dark over that tree root. Drunk as he was, the fall knocked him out completely.'

'I see. Let's go inside.'

While the constables were pushing the six-fold lattice doors of the main hall open, fragments of mouldering wood came down on their heads. Judge Dee went up the three broad stone stairs, stepped over the high threshold, and looked curiously at the cavernous, half-dark hall. On the right and left a row of six heavy stone pillars supported the thick rafters high above, from which dust-laden cobwebs hung down like so many grey pennons. At the far end, against the back wall, the judge saw vaguely an altar table of solid ebony, more than twelve feet long and about five feet high. In the side wall was a small narrow door, and above it, high up in the wall, a square window, boarded up with planks. Pointing at the window, Judge Dee asked, 'Can't your men open that, headman? It's too dark in here!'

At a sign from the headman two constables went to a niche in the wall behind the left row of pillars. They took two halberds from it. With those they set to work on the boarded-up window. While they were busy, Judge Dee walked on to the centre of the hall and silently surveyed it, slowly caressing his long sidewhiskers. The clammy, oppressive air seemed to clog up his lungs. Except for the holes bored at regular intervals in the wall for placing burning torches in, there was nothing left to suggest the orgies that had taken place there years ago, yet the hall emanated a subtle atmosphere of evil. Suddenly the judge had the uncanny feeling that unseen eyes were fixing him with a hostile stare.

'They say that formerly the walls were hung with large coloured pictures, Your Honour,' the headman spoke up beside him. 'Of naked gods and goddesses, and—'

'I am not interested in hearsay!' Judge Dee snapped.

45

Seeing the leer freeze on the headman's face, he asked, more friendly, 'Where do you think those ashes on the floor behind the pillars come from, headman?'

'In winter, Your Honour, the scum that frequent this place burn faggots here. They come to stay here overnight, especially during the cold months, for the thick walls protect them against rain and snow.'

'The heap of ashes here in the centre looks quite recent, though,' the judge remarked. The ashes were lying in a shallow round cavity, hollowed out in one of the flagstones. Around the cavity a wreath of lotus petals had been carved into the stone. The judge noticed that this particular flagstone was located in the exact centre of the floor. The eight flags surrounding it were marked by incised letters of a foreign script.

The boards that had covered the window at the back of the hall fell down with a thud. Two black shapes hurtled down from the rafters. One came flapping past Judge Dee's head with an eerie, piercing screech. Then the bats made for the dark cavity over the front entrance.

Sergeant Hoong had been studying the floor in front of the altar table. He righted himself and said, 'Now that we have better light, sir, you can see clearly that there was a veritable pool of blood here. But the thick layer of dust and refuse has absorbed it. And there are so many confused footprints all over that it's hard to draw any conclusions.'

Judge Dee went over to him and examined the floor. 'No, Heaven knows what happened here! Headman, get your men around me!' When the constables were standing in a half-circle in front of him, the judge resumed, 'I have information to the effect that, before or after the murder, a large wooden box was concealed inside this temple, or in the grounds outside. We shall begin inside.

46

I'll take the left wing with Sergeant Hoong and three men, the headman takes the right with the others. It must have been a fairly large box, so look for hidden cupboards, stone flags that show signs of having been taken up recently, trap doors and so on. Get to work!'

Two constables opened the door beside the niche for the ritual weapons. Besides the two long halberds which they had put back there, the niche contained one Tartar double axe, an exact replica of the murder weapon. They entered a narrow corridor about twenty-five feet long, with four door-openings on either side. These proved to give access to long, narrow rooms, each lit by a gaping window; the paper-covered latticework had disappeared long ago.

'Evidently these rooms were the cells of the priests,' the judge remarked. 'There must be a similar set of eight cells over in the right wing, for the groundplan of this temple is exactly symmetrical. Hey, come here, you!' Pointing at the tiled floor, Judge Dee told the constable: 'See whether you can pry those tiles loose. They don't seem to fit closely. Your two colleagues can inspect the floors of the cells opposite.'

The constable inserted the point of his knife in the groove between the flagstones. Three could be raised easily.

'See what was buried there!'

The man dug with his knife in the loose earth but there was nothing underneath except the solid stones of the temple's foundations.

'We are hot on the scent, sir!' Hoong exclaimed, excited. 'Someone wanted to bury something bulky here, but gave up when he found he couldn't make the hole deep enough!'

'Exactly, Hoong. We can skip the other cells. The

47

murderer will have gone on to the tower, to see whether there's a hollow space under the floor. He—'

'Come and have a look, please, Your Honour!' another constable said. 'Half of the floor in the cell opposite has been taken up!'

They quickly followed him. Six tiles in the centre of the cell had been removed and neatly piled up in the corner. Judge Dee rubbed his finger over the one on top: it was covered with a thin film of dust. 'Let's have a look at the other cells, men!'

They found that the floor of every single cell had been tampered with. In some cells the tiles had been neatly replaced, in others they had been carelessly thrown into a corner.

'On to the tower!' the judge ordered. He passed through the door-opening at the end of the corridor and entered the spacious octagonal hall that constituted the ground floor of the west tower. Here the floor had not been tampered with.

'Stands to reason,' Judge Dee muttered. 'These slabs are fixed into a layer of cement. You need a pickaxe to make a hole here. But look at the wainscoting!'

In several places the mouldering wooden boards that covered the brick wall had been torn down, disclosing an intervening space of about two inches.

'I don't understand why . . .' the sergeant began, perplexed.

'I do,' the judge interrupted gruffly. 'You inspect the staircase and the two floors above, men. Come along, Sergeant! We'll climb up to the top, to get some fresh air!'

They went up the creaking stairs, carefully stepping round the holes that gaped where a mouldering step had dropped out.

48

A narrow balcony went around the tower's top floor, under the overhanging eaves of the pointed roof. Judge Dee stood at the low balustrade. Folding his hands in his wide sleeves, he stared at the mass of green treetops below. After a while he turned to the sergeant and said, with a smile:

'Sorry that I was so short with you downstairs, Hoong. This is really a most vexing case. Now we have obtained our first clue, but that seems to have no bearing at all upon our murder! This temple was searched, and very thoroughly too. But not for a place to hide a body and a severed head, and not yesterday, but some time ago. The object of the search was something small, not larger than a few inches square, I'd say.'

The sergeant nodded slowly. Then he asked, 'How do you know that the object they were looking for was so small, sir?'

'Well, when the searcher had lifted the tiles in the first cell, and found that the layer of earth underneath was only five or six inches thick, he examined the floor of every other cell, hoping to find something buried there. Then he went on to search the empty space behind the wainscoting, and that is only a few inches from the brick wall, as you saw just now.' He thought a few moments, then resumed: 'I also think that the search was conducted independently by two different persons. One had much experience in this work; he tried to cover up his searching by carefully replacing the tiles. The other didn't care, he just threw the discarded tiles into a corner, and tore down the wainscoting.'

'You said that this search for a hidden object has no bearing on our case, sir. But we know that Seng-san used to frequent this temple. There might be a link between the murder and the search, even though the

49

search took place long before the murder was committed.'

'Yes, you are right, Hoong! That's a possibility we must seriously consider. Perhaps Seng-san and the other man were murdered because they found what a second party had been looking for in vain!' He considered for a while, stroking his long beard. 'As to our missing body and severed head, we won't find those inside. You'll have noticed that there isn't a drop of blood anywhere, nor any signs of blood having been wiped up.' He pointed at the treetops below. 'The obvious place to look for those remains is in that wilderness there. Quite a job, for from here you can see clearly how large the temple grounds are. Well, we'd better go down again.'

The three constables who had been inspecting the floors below reported that they had found no traces of a search having been conducted there. The walls had no wainscoting, and the bricks had not been tampered with.

The headman was standing in the hall, wiping his dirt-smeared, moist face with his neckcloth. His men were standing around him, talking in whispers.

'Someone has been tampering with the floors and the walls, sir,' he reported with a crestfallen look. 'But we didn't find any sign of a large box.'

'It must have been buried somewhere in the garden, headman. By the way, where does that narrow door near the altar over there lead to? I saw no back gate in the surrounding wall when I was standing on the top floor of the west tower.'

'The door leads to the narrow space behind the hall, Your Honour. Formerly there was a gate in the wall, but it has been bricked up for many years.'

'All right. Take all your men to the garden. Look for a spot where some digging has been done recently. In

50

the meantime we shall pay a visit to the Hermitage, Sergeant.'

While crossing the front yard, Judge Dee said, 'The murderer must have had an accomplice, Hoong. To drag Seng-san's body all the way outside, smear blood on Ah-liu's jacket, then bury the body and the other man's head somewhere in that dense wilderness—that isn't exactly a one-man job! Two murderers, and no motive! I don't like this at all, Hoong.'

They passed through the triple gate and took the foot-path running along the front of the temple's outer wall.

Judge Dee resumed: 'In times of political unrest, Buddhist monks often bury golden statues and other valuable objects of worship in order to prevent their being stolen. If there should be such a buried treasure in this deserted temple, then we would have a sound motive. The only trouble is that I have never heard a buried treasure mentioned in connection with this particular place!'

'Perhaps someone happened to discover a note about that in some old, forgotten record, sir.'

'Yes, there's a lot in that, Hoong! Suppose that the man then engaged three or four scoundrels to help him to make a secret search for the hidden treasure? If Seng-san and the other man were among them, and tried to keep the whole loot for themselves, that would give the others a good motive for murdering them. This theory would establish a logical link between the search and the murders.'

The path entered the wooded patch between the temple and the Hermitage. The judge halted and turned round.

'From here we have a good view of the entire temple. The hill goes down rather steeply directly behind the back wall. That's why the path leading down to the high-

51

way makes all those sharp turns. We must try to learn more about the history of the temple, Hoong. When we are back in the tribunal, I want you to investigate the old files in the chancery. Find out when exactly the authorities ordered the inmates to evacuate the temple, who the Abbot was and where he went, and whether there was ever any rumour about buried treasure.'

After a few minutes' walk through the forest they saw the neatly plastered wall of the Hermitage, a small one-storeyed temple built in purely Chinese style. The roof was decked with green-glazed tiles; the curved ridge ended in upturned points shaped like dragon-tails. They heard faintly the quacking of ducks. Except for that there was only the constant drone of the cicadas.

Sergeant Hoong rattled the knocker of polished copper on the red-lacquered gate. After he had repeated this several times, the peephole opened and a girl's face appeared behind the grating. She studied the two visitors suspiciously with her large, alert eyes, then asked sharply :

'What do you want?'

'We are from the tribunal,' the sergeant told her. 'Open up!'

The girl admitted them to a small paved yard. Evidently she was the maid, for she wore a simple dark-blue jacket and wide trousers of the same material. Judge Dee noticed that she had a common but rather pretty face; there were dimples in her round cheeks. The grey flag-stones of the yard were scrupulously clean and had been sprinkled with water to keep the air cool. On the left stood a small building of red brick, on the right a larger one with a veranda. The walls of the temple hall at the back were plastered a spotless white and the pillars supporting the curved eaves were lacquered red. Beside the well in the corner stood a rack carrying a row of potted plants, and on the highest shelf a few porcelain vases with tastefully arranged flowers. The judge recognized the style of flower arrangement practised by his wives and guessed that these were the work of the Abbess. The subtle fragrance of orchids drifted in the air. The judge reflected that, after the deserted temple, these refined surroundings were a pleasant change indeed.

'Well,' the girl asked impatiently, 'what can I do for you, sir?'

'Take my visiting-card to the Abbess,' Judge Dee said, groping in his sleeve.

'The Abbess is sleeping,' she said sullenly. 'Tonight she has to go to the city, to attend a party in the magistrate's residence. If you insist, I shall . . .'

'Oh no,' Judge Dee said quickly. 'I came only to inquire whether you heard or saw anything unusual last night. Some vagabonds were making trouble in the deserted temple. About midnight.'

'About midnight?' she scoffed. Indicating the buildings with a sweeping gesture, she went on: 'All this I have to keep clean, all alone by myself, mind you! It's a very small temple, but there are a lot of knick-knacks on the altar that need to be dusted. Do you think I feel like sitting up late at night after a day's hard work?'

'Do you also do all the shopping?' the judge asked curiously. 'If you have to go up and down that staircase every day—'

'I go only once a week for the soy, salt and beancurd. We don't eat meat or fish—worse luck!'

'I hear the quacking of ducks, though.'

Her face softened.

'Those are mine. The Abbess lets me keep them, for the

eggs. They are ever so cute, the small ones. . . .' She checked herself and asked curtly, 'Anything else I can do for you?'

'Not at this time. Come along, Hoong. Let's see how things are progressing at the temple.'

'What a pert young hussy!' the sergeant remarked when they were walking through the wood again.

The judge shrugged his shoulders.

'She's fond of ducks, and that is something, at least. Well, I am glad to have seen the Hermitage. The elegant atmosphere confirms the high opinion my ladies have of the Abbess.'

The headman and two constables were sitting on the steps of the main hall, looking hot and dishevelled. They jumped up when they saw Judge Dee enter the courtyard.

'No use, Your Honour! I'd swear that no one has been into that accursed wilderness over there for a long, long time! There isn't even a pathway. And there are no traces of any digging that we could see. The other men are still trying to get through by skirting the outer wall.'

Judge Dee sat down on a large boulder in the shadow of the wall and began to fan himself vigorously.

'You mentioned that the murderer must have had an accomplice, sir,' the sergeant said after a while. 'Couldn't they have put the body on an improvised stretcher and carried it down the hill?'

'Possible, but not very probable. They would have run the risk of meeting other vagabonds, and those are very inquisitive folk. The garden is our best bet, I think.'

One by one the constables emerged from the garden. They shook their heads.

54

The judge rose.

'It's getting late. We'd better go back to the tribunal. Seal the doors of the hall, headman. Leave two men here to guard the place. And see to it that they are relieved at nightfall.'

VII

Ma Joong had put on a pair of wide trousers and a patched jacket of faded blue cotton, and bound up his hair with a red rag. In that disreputable attire he would attract no undue attention in the north-west city ward, the quarter assigned to the Tartars, Indians, Uigurs and other foreign barbarians.

It was a long walk, but he made good progress, for most of the shops were closed for the afternoon siesta and there were few people about. After he had passed the Drum Tower, however, the narrow streets became more lively: having hurriedly gobbled down their noodles at noon, the poor people living there had at once to set to work again, to scrape together the few coppers for their evening meal.

Picking his way through the motley crowd of Central-Asian coolies and Chinese hawkers jostling one another in the smelly back streets, he at last reached the alley where Tulbee had established her soup kitchen. He saw her from afar, standing in front of the oven and scolding her elder boy, who was stirring the fire under the huge iron cauldron. Her other boy was clinging to her skirt. It was too early yet for customers. He sauntered up to her.

'Ma Joong!' she cried out happily. 'How nice to see

you again! But you look like nothing on earth! Has your boss kicked you out? I always told you that you are far too good a man to serve as thief-catcher. You should—'

'Hush!' he interrupted. 'I am dressed up like this because I am on a job.'

'Let go, you small devil!' she shouted, boxing the ears of the younger boy, who obstinately clung to her skirt. He promptly began to bawl at the top of his voice. His brother gave Ma Joong a scornful look, then spat into the fire. Ma Joong noticed the all too familiar smell of rancid butter, and he saw that her nose wasn't clean. She was getting fat too. He sent up a silent prayer of thanks to the merciful Heaven for having spared him all this! He groped in his sleeve and brought out a string of coppers. 'This—' he began. But she raised her hand and said, pouting:

'Shame on you, Ma Joong! You offering me money for it, you of all people!' But she put the coppers in her sleeve anyway, and went on: 'My husband is away for the day, so we can have a nice long chat up in my room. The boys'll mind the shop and—'

'I told you I am out on a job!' he said quickly. 'The money is for information received, as they say! Let's sit down on that bench there.'

'Come along up!' she said, grabbing his hand with a determined expression. 'You'll get your information, garnished! It's nice to be out of the business, of course, but . . . well, there's something in variety too. And you know how I feel about you, Ma Joong!' She cast a meaningful look at the door.

He pressed her down on the bench and took a seat close by her.

'Next time, dear. I am in a hurry, honestly! I am sup-

57

posed to find out about a quarrel some of your people had with Seng-san, that's a bully from the quarter near the east gate. A real bad quarrel, you know. Seng-san got his head chopped off.'

'Our boys don't mix with Chinese riff-raff,' she said sullenly. 'How could they, not understanding each other's language?' Brightening up, she asked, 'You remember how you used to teach me Chinese, Ma Joong?'

'I certainly do!' he said, grinning in spite of himself. 'Well, I am not saying your people did anything bad, mind you. My boss just wants to prevent further trouble; he likes to keep an orderly house, as they say in the business. Come on, think girl! Didn't you overhear your customers mention a fight in the old temple, outside the east gate?'

She pensively picked her nose. Then she said, slowly, 'The only big thing I heard of recently is the killing of a Tartar chieftain, over the border. In settlement of a blood-feud.' She gave him a sidelong glance and added, 'Your mentioning a temple reminded me of something. Four streets down lives a weird woman, a Tartar sorceress. Tala, her name is. A real witch, knows past and future. If ever one of our people wants to start something big, he consults her first. She knows everything, Ma Joong, absolutely everything! But that doesn't mean she tells what she knows! The people are getting sour with her, nowadays. They maintain she gives out wrong advice, perhaps on purpose. If they weren't so afraid of her, they'd. . . .' She slit her forefinger across her throat.

'How do I get there?'

'Stop meddling with that oven!' Tulbee shouted at her eldest son. 'Take Mr Ma to Tala!' As Ma Joong rose she whispered, quickly: 'Look sharp, Ma Joong! It's a bad neighbourhood!'

58

MA JOONG MEETS AN OLD GIRL FRIEND

'I'll take good care of myself! Thanks ever so much!'

The crooked alley the boy took him to was lined by one-storeyed houses with sagging mud walls and roughly-made thatched roofs. After he had pointed out a somewhat larger house half-way down that had a pointed roof vaguely reminiscent of a Tartar tent, the boy scurried away. The only people about were three Tartars, squatting with their backs against the wall opposite the house of the sorceress. They wore baggy leather trousers with broad belts; their muscular torsos were bare. The midday sun shone on their round heads, closely shaven but for one long lock of hair at the back. When Ma Joong passed them, one said in broken Chinese to his companions, 'She even receives Chinese scum nowadays!'

Studiously ignoring the insult, Ma Joong pulled the greasy door-curtain aside. In the dark interior he vaguely discerned two shapes huddled over a small fire that was burning in a hole in the floor of stamped earth. Since they didn't pay the slightest attention to him, he sat down on a low stool just inside the door opening. He couldn't see much, for his eyes had not yet adjusted themselves after the glare of the sun outside. The cool air was scented with an outlandish incense that reminded him of a pharmacy; he thought it might be camphor wood. The hooded figure squatting with her back towards him kept up a long monologue in a foreign, guttural tongue. It was old crone, clad in a Tartar felt coat. The woman facing her on the other side of the fire seemed to be seated on a low chair. He couldn't make out her shape, for she was entirely enveloped in a long, shapeless cloak that hung from her shoulders down to the floor. Her head was bare; a mass of long, black hair cascaded down over her shoulders and half screened her downcast face. The sorceress was listening to the voice of the old crone, which droned on and on.

Ma Joong folded his arms. Settling down for a long wait, he surveyed the scanty furnishings. Against the wall behind the sorceress stood a low, roughly-made plank bed, flanked by two bamboo tabourets. On one stood a brass hand-bell with a long, elaborately moulded handle. From the wall above the bed two large rolling eyes stared down at him. They belonged to a more than lifesize picture of a fierce god, painted in full colours. His long hair stood on end, forming a kind of nimbus round the large head. One arm brandished a strange-looking ritual weapon; in his left hand he held a cup made of a human skull. The obese red body was naked but for a tiger skin wound round the loins. A writhing snake hung round his shoulders. Was it the effect of the flickering fire, or did the gaping mouth with the lolling tongue move in a derisive sneer? He got a fleeting impression that it wasn't a picture at all, but a statue. He couldn't be sure, for behind the monstrous deity there were only dark shadows.

Annoyed, he averted his eyes from the repulsive sight and scanned the rest of the room. In the far corner lay a heap of rubbish. Animal skins were piled up against the side wall, beside it stood a large water container of beaten brass. Feeling increasingly ill at ease, he drew his jacket closer round his shoulders, for it was actually getting chilly now. Trying to think of other, more pleasant, things, he reflected that Tulbee wasn't so bad, after all. He ought to look her up some day and take her a few presents. Then he thought of the woman called Jade, and of her mysterious message which they had found in the ebony box. Had she been saved after all, and where could she be now? Jade was a beautiful name, suggesting cool, aloof beauty. . . . He had a feeling that she was a most desirable woman. . . . He looked up. The voice of the old crone had ceased at last.

A white hand appeared from the folds of the cloak enveloping the sorceress. She stirred up the fire with a thin stick, then drew with the red-glowing tip a few diagrams in the ashes, whispering to the crone. The old woman nodded eagerly. She laid a few greasy coppers beside the fire, scrambled up with a grunt and disappeared through the felt door-curtain.

Ma Joong went to get up to introduce himself, but the sorceress lifted her head, and he sat down again abruptly. Two large, burning eyes were staring at him. The same eyes that had glared at him that morning in the street. She had a very beautiful but cold face, and her bloodless lips were curved in a disdainful sneer.

'Did you come to inquire whether your girl still loves you, Mr Official?' she asked in a deep throaty voice. 'Or did your boss send you to find out whether I am practising witchcraft, forbidden by your laws?' She spoke faultless Chinese. As Ma Joong stared at her, dumbfounded, she continued: 'I saw you, Mr Official, all dressed up. This morning, when you were following your boss, the bearded judge.'

'You have sharp eyes!' Ma Joong muttered. He drew his stool up closer to the fire which was burning low. He was at a loss how to begin.

'Speak up, what brought you here? I haven't been receiving stolen goods. See for yourself!'

She stirred up the fire, and pointed with the stick at the corner.

Ma Joong gasped. What he had taken for a heap of rubbish now turned out to be a pile of human bones. Two skulls seemed to grin at him with their toothy mouths.

On top of the skins lay a row of human thighbones beside a broken pelvis, blackened by age.

'A blasted cemetery!' he exclaimed, horrified.

'Aren't we living in a cemetery, everywhere and always?' Tala scoffed. 'The living are outnumbered by the dead by uncounted myriads. We, the living, are here on sufferance. Better keep on good terms with the dead, Mr Official! Now, what is your business?'

Ma Joong took a deep breath. There was no need to beat about the bush with this extraordinary woman. So he said curtly: 'A vagabond named Seng-san was murdered last night, outside the east gate. He—'

'You are wasting your time,' she interrupted. 'I only know what is happening here in this quarter. And across the border. I know nothing about what happens at the other end of the city. If, however, you want to know about the girl you were thinking of just now, I might be able to help you.' Seeing his bewildered look, she went on quickly: 'Not the little strumpet called Tulbee, Mr Official. I mean the other one, named after a precious stone.'

'If you know . . . who Jade is, and where . . .' Ma Joong stammered.

'I don't. But I shall ask my husband.'

She rose and shook the cloak from her shoulders. Ma Joong got another shock. Her tall, perfect body was stark naked.

He gaped at her, paralysed by a deep-rooted, nameless terror. For the pale, completely hairless shape seemed so unreal, so far remote from ordinary life that its generous curves, far from rousing his desire, made him shrink with fear, the abject fear of the unknown. When, with a tremendous effort he succeeded in averting his eyes, he saw that she had not been sitting on a chair, but on a small pyramid of skulls.

63

'Yes,' she said, in her cold, impersonal voice, 'this is the beginning. Shorn of all your stupid day-dreams, of all your cherished illusions.' Pointing at the heap of skulls, she added : 'And this is the end, shorn of all empty promises and all fond hope.' She kicked the pile over with her bare foot. The skulls rolled rattling over the floor.

For a while she stood looking down at him with infinite scorn, her arms akimbo, her legs spread. Cold sweat broke out all over him as he sat cowering there. As if in a dream, he watched her as she turned round abruptly and undid a cord from an iron hook in the wall. A screen of painted cloth that had been fastened to the blackened rafters slowly descended. It divided the room into two compartments. She shook her hair and disappeared behind the screen.

The fire seemed to be dying out. He had not understood the full meaning of her words, but they filled him with a terrible feeling of utter loneliness. He stared fixedly at the strange symbols depicted on the screen, his mind frozen. Suddenly the sharp tinkling of the brass bell roused him from his mental stupor. Tala began to intone a monotonous chant in a strange language. First it rose, then it died out, to be revived again by the tinkling of the bell. It grew warmer in the room, and at the same time a nauseating smell of decay drowned the clean fragrance of the camphor wood. Gradually it became hot; sweat was streaming down his back, drenching his jacket. Suddenly the chant changed into a low moaning sound. The tinkling of the bell ceased. He balled his large fists in impotent rage, his nails cutting his calloused palms. His stomach was turning.

Just when he thought he was going to be violently sick, the air suddenly cleared. The clean smell of camphor superseded the foul stench and it grew less hot

64

THE CONSORT OF A GOD

in the room. For some time all was quiet as the grave. Then her voice came from behind the screen, utterly weary:

'Raise the screen and fasten the cord.'

He rose stiffly and did as she had said, not daring to look at her. When he had tied the cord to the hook and turned round, he saw her lying stretched out on the plank bed, her head on her arm, her eyes closed. Her long hair hung down to the floor.

'Come here!' she ordered without opening her eyes.

He sat down on the bamboo stool at the foot of the bed. He saw that her body was covered with a thin film of sweat. Her lower lip was bleeding.

'Your girl Jade was born twenty years ago, on the fourth day of the fifth month of the year of the Mouse. She died last year on the tenth day of the ninth month. The year of the Snake. Of a broken neck.'

'How . . . who did . . . ?' Ma Joong began.

'That was all I was told. I was told also about myself. Unasked for. Go away!'

With an effort he mustered his courage.

'I must order you to give me more details. Otherwise I shall have to take you to the tribunal, to . . .'

She languidly stretched out her hand, still without looking at him.

'Show me your warrant!'

As Ma Joong did not answer, she suddenly raised her drooping eyelids. He saw that her eyes were bloodshot, they looked broken, dead.

Ma Joong retched. He jumped up and made for the door. Half-blinded by the sun, he bumped into a lean shape. It was one of the Tartars. The three were standing in the street now, barring his way. The tallest gave him a push.

66

'Watch out, son of a dog! Did you have a good time with the witch?'

All his pent-up fear and frustration burst out. He felled the Tartar with a blow to his chin so ferocious that the man pitched over like a log of wood. The two others ran away as fast as they could: they had recognized in Ma Joong's blazing eyes the killer's look. He ran after them, in a blind rage. The people in the street further on quickly made way for the cursing giant. Then he stepped into a hole and fell down flat on his face. When he had slowly scrambled to his feet again, he saw that he was in Tulbee's street.

She was standing in front of her kitchen, stirring the cauldron with a long ladle. Looking over her shoulder, she was cursing in a strident voice her eldest boy, who was pulling the hair of his shrieking small brother.

Ma Joong's rage ebbed away. That homely, common-place scene made a warm, comfortable feeling rise in his breast. He saw from the position of the sun that it was still early in the afternoon. First a bowl of hot soup, to settle his stomach. . . . He quickly wiped the mud from his face and walked up to her with a broad smile.

VIII

All the lamps were burning brightly in the large dining-room of Judge Dee's residence, and a bevy of maids were hanging garlands of coloured lampions on the low branches of the trees in the front garden. The First Lady, in a long-sleeved robe of shimmering violet brocade embroidered with gold, was seeing off the last lady guest from her tea party. After she had made her final bow, she cast an anxious glance at the back gate of the chancery. The housemaster had told her that the judge had come back from the temple an hour before, but he had not yet made his appearance. Turning to the Third Lady, who looked very fragile in her rustling long robe of stiff white gauze, she said, 'I do hope our husband will come in time to receive the Abbess! Dinner will start in an hour!'

The conference in Judge Dee's private office was nearing its end. The judge was leaning back in his armchair, slowly combing his long black beard with outspread fingers. The light of the silver candlestick shone on his drawn face. Sergeant Hoong sat huddled on the bamboo chair in the corner, tired after the hot afternoon in the temple and the long search in the dusty chancery archives afterwards. His thin hands were in his lap, folding and unfolding mechanically his sheet of notes. Ma Joong,

68

sitting opposite the judge, was looking glum. After the judge had told him about the search of the deserted temple, Ma Joong had reported his visit to the sorceress, and Judge Dee had made him repeat their conversation word for word. Although his prolonged session with Tulbee had rid him of the haunting fear that he could never love a woman again, the recounting of the harrowing interview with Tala had upset him more than he cared to admit.

At last Judge Dee spoke:

'As to the general remarks of that woman Tala, I prefer not to go further into those. They refer to a perfidious teaching that foully debases what any decent man holds most sacred. As to her astonishing references to the girl named Jade, her knowing that you are concerned with her is easily explained, Ma Joong. While waiting for the sorceress to finish with the old crone, you were concentrating your thoughts on Jade. And Tala, like most women of her strange profession, evidently possesses the faculty of reading other people's thoughts—up to a certain point, of course. Part of their success as soothsayers depends on that faculty. As to how she knew the dates of Jade's birth and alleged demise, I wouldn't even hazard a guess.'

'Let's arrest the awful woman and beat the truth out of her!' Ma Joong burst out.

Judge Dee took an official form from the pile on his desk and filled it out with his red writing-brush. After he had impressed the large seal of the tribunal on it, he said, shaking his head, 'It is indeed my duty to try to arrest her. But I haven't the faintest hope that we shall succeed. She fully realizes, of course, that a warrant for her arrest will be issued. Even now she may be crossing the frontier into Tartar territory! Especially since her own people in

69

the north-west quarter are turning against her. Anyway, give this paper to the headman, Ma Joong, and explain to him where Tala lives!'

After Ma Joong had gone, the sergeant asked, 'Why should she have given Ma Joong that information, sir?'

'I haven't the slightest idea, Hoong! At any rate, we know now that the message in the ebony box can't have been a complete hoax. As to its real meaning, though . . .' His voice trailed off. He stared sombrely at the ebony box, which he was using as a paper-weight. The polished jade disc shone in the light of the candle with a malignant gleam.

Tugging at his moustache he let his eyes wander towards the pile of dossiers on his desk, but every time they came back again to the ebony box.

When Ma Joong returned, Judge Dee sat up in his chair.

'Take a brush and a piece of paper, Ma Joong,' he said curtly. 'Write down what I shall dictate you.' After his lieutenant had moistened the writing-brush, the judge went on: 'Anyone who can supply information about the full name and present whereabouts of a woman called Jade who disappeared in the ninth month of the year of the Snake, is urgently requested to report to this tribunal at his earliest convenience. Magistrate Dee. That is all, Ma Joong. Take it to the chancery, and order the clerks to write it out a few dozen times, to be posted this very night throughout the city. Putting up this proclamation is the best I can do with regard to the vexing puzzle of the ebony box.'

He sat back in his chair again and told the sergeant briskly, 'Tell Ma Joong what you have learned about the deserted temple!'

Hoong drew his chair closer to the candle. He consulted the paper on his lap and began: 'The Temple of the Purple Clouds was built two hundred and eighty years ago by Indian monks, the funds being provided by the local foreign community, which was greatly prospering at that time. The temple suffered various misfortunes during the border wars but the religious services were never interrupted for long. Thirty years ago, however, three priests of the new creed arrived from over the border, accompanied by three nuns. Having settled down in the temple, they converted some of the inmates; the others left in disgust and were replaced by new converts, some Tartar, some Chinese. The new creed was spreading like wildfire among the barbarians, and the foreign population of this district visited the temple in crowds. Then, about fifteen years ago, some leading citizens lodged a complaint with this tribunal, denouncing the obscene rituals conducted in the temple. The magistrate instituted a close inquiry. As a result the Abbot was sent in chains to the capital, all the pictures, statues and other paraphernalia were publicly burned in the market, and the inmates banished.'

'Good man!' Judge Dee said approvingly. 'That's the only way to deal with such excesses.'

The sergeant glanced at his notes and resumed: 'These stern measures created unrest among the Tartar population; there was even an attempt at armed rebellion. To placate the excited people, the magistrate allowed one Chinese priest and one Tartar priestess who had recanted to build the Hermitage and to practise there the old Buddhist ritual approved by the authorities. However, the number of visitors dwindled. After a few years the priestess left, and some time after the priest also went away. The authorities sealed the Hermitage. Two years ago, the highway to the tributary kingdoms of the west was moved from Lan-fang up north, and the foreign population of Lan-fang shrunk. Last year the magistrate planned to close down the Hermitage permanently. Then, however, the well-known goldsmith Chang suddenly died, leaving no offspring. His widow, who had always been a fervent Buddhist, became a nun and requested that the Hermitage be assigned to her. The Hermitage was dedicated in the autumn of the year of the Snake, on the twentieth day of the ninth month. That is all.'

'A rather interesting story, Ma Joong,' Judge Dee commented. 'But it doesn't shed any light on our problem. I had hoped for data on old buried treasure there.' He sighed. For a while silence reigned in the small, hot office. Then Ma Joong pushed his cap back and said:

'Since my trip to the north-west quarter didn't produce any data regarding the murder, what about my trying the neighbourhood of the east gate tonight, sir? There are a lot of cheap eating-houses and taverns. Seng-san was a well-known underworld figure, it won't be difficult to locate people there who knew him well, and make them talk about him.'

'Do that,' the judge said. 'There must be a Head of the Beggars here, and he will know much about what's going on in the underworld. Have a talk with him too, Ma Joong.'

'Then, as regards the missing head and body, sir, I too believe they were buried in the temple garden. The headman and the constables searched it, but I can tell you from my experience in the "green woods" that in the dark a forest looks completely different. The constables may well have overlooked in broad daylight features that spring to the eye at night. I would like to go there tonight, sir, to have a look around. See the situation through the eyes of the murderer, so to speak.'

The judge nodded slowly. 'There's a lot in what you say, Ma Joong. All right, have a try! I put two constables on guard there and they can help by clearing a path for you. Don't forget to put on thick leggings, for I am told there are poisonous snakes.' He rose. 'Well, I shall now take a quick bath and change for the festive dinner.'

Half an hour later Judge Dee entered the main dining-room, clad in his ceremonial robe of gold-embroidered green brocade and wearing his high black cap. He was just in time. His First Lady was leading the Abbess in through the front entrance, followed by his Second and Third Ladies.

The judge hastily went to meet the Abbess. Making a bow, he bade her welcome to his residence. She bowed three times in succession, her hands folded in the long sleeves of her wide, saffron-coloured robe. Modestly keeping her eyes down, she thanked the judge in a few well-chosen words for his kind invitation. He regarded her curiously, for up to now he had only got occasional glimpses of her tall figure when she was crossing the yard to his women's quarters to give her lessons in flower arrangement. Knowing that she was about forty, he thought she was still rather good-looking, in a cold, rather austere way. Her head and shoulders were covered by a black hood that left the oval of her face free. He noticed the high, curved nose, and the thin, determined mouth.

The five of them sat down on low tabourets of carved sandalwood at the square marble corner table. The six-fold lattice doors had been opened wide to let in the cool evening air. From where they were sitting they had a fine view of the front garden, where the gaily coloured paper lanterns lit up the dark-green foliage. While two maids filled their cups with fragrant jasmine tea, another placed platters with candied fruit and dried melon seeds on the table. The four women waited respectfully for the judge to open the conversation.

'I must warn Your Reverence in advance,' he began, 'that tonight's dinner is only a small family affair. I can only hope that our simple fare won't seem wholly devoid of taste to you.'

'It is the company rather than the fare that sets the tone of a gathering, Excellency,' the Abbess said gravely. 'I must offer my humble apologies for the extremely rude behaviour of my maid this afternoon. She ought to have informed me at once of Your Excellency's arrival, of course. She's a stupid, uneducated girl from down town. I chastised her, but . . .' She raised her plump hand in a resigned gesture. The crystal beads of the rosary round her right wrist made a tinkling sound.

'It didn't matter at all!' Judge Dee assured her. 'I just wanted to check whether you had been bothered by vagabonds who made trouble in the deserted temple last night. The maid told me that in the Hermitage nothing special was seen or heard.'

The Abbess raised her head and fastened her large, vacant eyes on the judge.

'The temple has been desecrated by heterodox rites, formerly practised there by misguided sectarians. But the Lord Buddha will in His infinite mercy bless also those apostates.' She stretched out her white hand and took a sip from her tea. 'As to my maid, I wonder whether she really told you all she knew.' As the judge raised his eyebrows, she went on: 'I suspect her of a lewd disposition. She is always trying to strike up acquaintance with the vagabonds that roam the woods. The other night I caught her

74

THE BIRTHDAY DINNER

talking and giggling with a wretched beggar right in front of the gate. I gave her a thorough caning, but I doubt whether that will help. I can only pray for her.' She began automatically to count the beads of the crystal rosary.

'You shouldn't keep that girl!' the First Lady exclaimed. Turning to the Second, she added: 'You'd better make inquiries among your Buddhist acquaintances. They might know a suitable girl for Her Reverence!'

The Second cast an apprehensive look at her husband. She had embraced Buddhism after their arrival in Lanfang. Having received only an elementary education, the simple teachings and the colourful ritual had appealed to her. Although the judge had raised no objections, she knew that he had not been too happy about her conversion. But Judge Dee's thoughts were elsewhere at the moment. The maid evidently sought to brighten up the dreary life in the Hermitage by associating with the vagabonds, and therefore she might be able to supply valuable information.

'I ordered my lieutenant Ma Joong to make a thorough search of the deserted temple tonight,' he told the Abbess. 'Perhaps he could call at the Hermitage and question your maidservant.'

'It would be better if she is interrogated in my presence, sir,' the Abbess said primly. 'If she's alone with your man, she might . . . eh, put him off.'

'Of course. I shall . . . Ha, there are the children!'

The nurse led Judge Dee's sons and his daughter into the hall. The youngest, a sturdy small boy of three, she carried in her arms. After the First Lady had presented them to the Abbess, the housemaster came to report that dinner was ready.

They went to the large round table at the other end of

76

the hall. The judge sat down at the head, directly in front of the carved ebony altar table against the back wall. Above the table hung the large character for 'long life' he had written at noon. He invited the Abbess to take the seat at his right, the First Lady sat down on his left, and the Second and Third took their places opposite them. The First Lady told the nurse to take the children back to their room, but the small boy had taken a fancy to the flowers stuck in her golden hairband and would not let go of them. So she said that the nurse could stay, standing behind her chair.

While they were tasting the cold entrées, the housemaster brought in the first warm dish of roasted bean-curd, and the eldest maid filled the wine-cups. Judge Dee raised his cup and gave a toast. Now the dinner had really begun.

IX

At approximately the same time that Judge Dee and his ladies sat down to dinner, Ma Joong walked up to the counter of a street stall selling cheap liquor behind the Temple of the War God. The two coolies sitting there quickly paid their coppers and left. The owner, a tall ruffian wearing a loose jacket that left his hairy breast bare, reached up and transferred the single oil-lamp that lit his stall from the front to the back.

Ma Joong understood. His official black cap marking him as a member of the tribunal frightened customers. He took a handful of coppers from his sleeve and placed them on the counter, at the same time ordering a drink. The owner stretched out his hand, but Ma Joong quickly put his large fist over the coppers.

'Slowly, my friend. You'll have to earn them! I want to talk to you about Seng-san. The fellow who was murdered last night. You know him?'

'Sure. That's another good customer gone! And he'd have become an even better customer shortly. Told me last week he was on to a big thing, with big money!'

'Something a foreign barbarian was mixed up with, eh?'

'Oh no! Seng-san wasn't what you'd call particular, but he drew the line at those blasted foreigners!'

78

'Who did he work for, then? He was all brawn and no brain, couldn't have managed a big affair single-handed.'

The other shrugged.

'Smelled like blackmail to me. And that Seng-san could handle by himself all right!'

'You know who he was blackmailing?'

'Not a hope! Seng-san was a big talker, but on this job he kept mum. Just said there was a pot of money in it.'

'Where did the bastard live?'

'Now here, now there. Often spent the night in the deserted temple of late. Have another drink?'

'No thank you. Perhaps the fellow he was blackmailing was staying in the temple too.'

'Are you crazy? Who would you blackmail there, I ask you? The white spook?' He spat on the ground.

'The Head of the Beggars might know. Who is that, nowadays?'

'Nobody. This is a hell of a city for a poor man to make a living, mister. First the henchmen of that bastard Chien Mow took all the businesses in their own dirty paws. Then that bearded son of a—I beg your pardon, the present magistrate, I meant to say, took over. And he keeps an eye on everything, all right! Heavens, that was old Chow who passed! Without giving me a second look. Listen, mister, do me a favour and walk on, will you? You're ruining my business. If you want to have a long and cosy talk, go and see the old King of the Beggars.'

Ma Joong pushed the coppers over to him.

'You just said there was no such man!'

'There isn't. Not any more. The King was a very tough customer, once. A real giant, of Tartar descent, I think. He was the boss of the underworld. But he's old now, and he's got trouble with his ticker. Lives somewhere in a cellar, I believe. Many thanks for the coppers, but don't come again, if you can help it!'

Ma Joong grunted something and walked on. He thought that blackmail might well have been the motive of the double murder. The object hidden in the temple might be a package of compromising letters. First the victim tried to recover them; then, when he failed, he killed the two blackmailers.

Ma Joong spent the next hour visiting four wine-houses. When he left the last one, he muttered, 'Wish Chiao Tai were with me! Makes the job much more pleasant when you have a friend you can talk to. Wonder what Brother Chiao is doing with himself in the capital. Having one more unlucky love affair, I wager! Well, I have drunk a lot of bad liquor, but I haven't learned a thing. Everybody agrees that Seng-san was a mean bully, and that he had no friends except for Ah-liu. I don't expect much from the so-called King of the Beggars either. Seems to be a pitiful old wreck. Ekes out a miserable existence with only one old fellow who used to be his chief henchman in the old days. I should—'

He looked round. A tall, lean man had overtaken him. It was the painter Lee Ko.

'What brings you to this part of the town, Mr Lee?'

'I am getting a bit worried about my assistant Yang, Mr Ma. Fellow hasn't turned up. He's been on a spree before, but then he always told me in advance. I am checking the taverns here. Where are you bound for?'

'The old temple on the hill. If you don't find Yang, let me know. The tribunal could make a few routine checks. So long!'

Ma Joong strolled on to the east city gate. He told the guards to lend him a small storm lantern, then he had a snack in one of the cheap eating-houses that lined the highway just outside the gate. After that he felt in the right mood for climbing the steep staircase. Now that night had fallen, it had become somewhat cooler. But the stiff climb still made him sweat profusely.

'I wonder why they must always build their blasted temples in such high places!' he muttered. 'To be nearer to Heaven, I suppose!'

When he stepped on to the clearing in front of the triple temple gate, two men came out from behind a cypress tree, swinging their clubs. Recognizing Ma Joong, they saluted and reported that he was the first visitor they had seen so far. He saw with satisfaction that one was Fang, an intelligent youngster.

'I am going to have a look around in the temple grounds,' he told the constables. 'Stay where you are. If I need you, I'll whistle. If you see a suspect character, you nab him and whistle for me.'

He passed through the gate and surveyed the front yard for a while. It looked bleak in the pale rays of the full moon.

'That garden on the left must indeed be the father and mother of all jungles!' he said to himself. 'Well, I'll do this properly. First I'll have a squint at the main hall; then I'll imagine I am a murderer with a corpse and a severed head on my hands!'

Going up the stairs of the main gate he found that, after Judge Dee's visit in the afternoon, the headman had sealed the six-fold doors. He tore the strip of paper down, and rattled the old, warped doors vigorously till he could push one panel open. About to enter the pitch-dark hall, he suddenly stood still. He had heard the sound of a door closing somewhere in the back of the hall. But now all was silent as the grave again. Suppressing a curse, he lit the lantern with his tinderbox and went inside, holding it high. The light shone on the heavy pillars and the massive altar table in the rear. He walked quickly to the small door to the left of the altar, for the sound seemed to have come from there. He pushed it open. Two steps went down into a long, narrow paved backyard. There was no one about.

'The headman ought to have sealed this door too, of course!' he grumbled. 'But probably I imagined hearing that sound.' He sniffed the air. Suddenly he felt alarmed. In the hall hung the same sickly stench of decay he had noticed in Tala's house. 'Heavens, suppose the corpse and head are hidden here in this very hall! The boss didn't make a search here, for the floor-tiles are all intact, and covered with dirt.' Raising the lantern above his head, he scanned the high rafters. 'What about that niche there over the entrance? You could get a corpse up there, if you had a ladder. And perhaps the murderer did have a ladder. There was plenty of time for doing the job, he had all night!'

He pulled the two central panels of the six-fold front door open. Having secured them in that position by wedging flat stones underneath, he suspended the lantern on his belt, grabbed the upper edge of the panel and climbed up, putting his feet in the gaps among the latticework. Standing with spread legs, one foot on either door, he could just look into the dark cavity. A black shape flew into his face and nearly made him lose his balance.

'Damn those bats! There's plenty of room here for a thousand of them, and for a couple of corpses too. But there's no corpse and no head. And it doesn't smell as badly here as down in the hall.'

He climbed down again and extinguished the lantern. Standing in the door-opening, he surveyed the thick wilderness along the right side of the yard.

'That big oak tree there with the raised roots must be the one beneath which our good Ah-liu laid himself down for a well-earned rest. All right, I sling the corpse over my shoulder and step down into the yard. The severed head I carry in my neckcloth. Or perhaps I entrust that precious burden to my friend. Then . . .'

He broke off and stared fixedly at the undergrowth, a little beyond the oak tree. He wiped his forehead.

'I'd have sworn I saw a white shape hovering about there! Could've been a woman. Rather tall, in a long, trailing white robe. After her!'

He ran across the yard. Beyond the oak tree, however, there was only a thick mass of thorny wild white roses.

'Where did the apparition . . .' he began, then stooped and looked at the broken twigs. When he had carefully parted the low branches, he grinned. 'Yes, there is a pathway here! Was, I should have said. Overgrown with weeds.'

Going down on all fours, he crept under the overhanging branches. Being an experienced woodsman, he knew that he was on an old footpath, hidden under the straggling undergrowth. Soon he could walk upright. He went on, hardly making any noise, halting from time to time to listen. But he heard nothing but the chirping of the cicadas, and the occasional cry of some night animal. He lit the lantern and examined the shrubs. There were dark stains on some leaves. He was on the right track.

The abandoned path meandered among the tall trees, on to a small clearing. Here another path branched off.

'That must lead back to the rear of the temple, I'd say. But I must keep to the left.' He sniffed the air. The dank smell of rotting leaves was being superseded by a subtle fragrance. 'Almond blossom! There must be several trees ahead!'

83

A little farther he came upon an old well, surrounded by tall almond trees. Their white blossoms were strewn over the mossy stones like so many snow flakes. Beyond the thick shrubbery on the other side of the well he saw a high wall. A large portion of the masonry had crumbled down, leaving a gap several feet wide. A pile of broken bricks and large boulders was lying beside the well, overgrown with weeds.

He looked up. Through the open space between the branches of the trees he could see the left tower of the deserted temple. That gave him his bearings.

'This abandoned well must be located in the farthest corner, at the back of this blasted garden. Where has my kind spook gone now? It either disappeared through the gap in the wall over there, or it took the side path I saw on the way here. Anyhow, she isn't here now, and that's a consolation!'

He was talking aloud to himself, for he felt far from comfortable. Supernatural phenomena were the only things under the sun he was actually afraid of. He scanned the dark trees, but nothing stirred. Shrugging his shoulders, he turned to the well.

'This is, of course, the ideal spot for dumping unwanted corpses. Yes, look at those dark stains on the rim! And down here along the bricks! Dark red!' He peeped inside. 'Very deep, more than twenty feet, I'd say. Lots of vegetation on the walls. This pitcher rope is rotten to the core, but it'll bear the weight of my lantern, I dare say.'

He tied the end of the rope to the handle and lowered it into the well. Under the mass of ivy there were thick liana stems that had worked their way deeply into the grooves among the old bricks. Large sections of the masonry had dropped out, leaving gaps all the way down. He peered intently at the bottom of the well.

MA JOONG MAKES A DISCOVERY

'Nothing but stones and high weeds!' he muttered, disappointed. 'Yet the corpse must be down there somewhere.' He quickly hauled the lantern up and hooked the handle under his belt. Then he climbed over the rim, took a firm hold on a thick liana stem, and groped about with his feet for a foothold in the wall. He was a trained athlete, but he had to watch his every move, for in many places the old bricks gave way when he put his foot on them. At last he had descended so far that he could let himself drop down among the weeds on the bottom. He quickly stepped aside, for his right foot had struck something soft. He stooped, and a pleased grin creased his face. It was a man's leg. Parting the weeds, he saw the stark naked, headless torso of a giant of a man, its tattooed back turned up.

Ma Joong squatted and let the light of the lantern fall on the complicated design decorating the man's back. It was tattooed in vivid green, blue and yellow colours.

'That must have cost him a pretty penny!' he thought. 'The large tiger mask between his shoulders must have been meant to protect him against attacks from behind. But the charm let him down this particular time. For he was killed by that knife-thrust just under the left shoulder blade. It's Seng-san all right! Look at those heavy muscles on his arms and legs. But where is the head of the other chap?'

He searched the limited circular space, but only discovered a bundle of blue clothes. At one place a large portion of the masonry had crumbled away, leaving a kind of shallow niche in the brick wall, about four feet high and three feet deep. Squatting, he let the light of the lantern fall inside. A large toad stared up at him, blinking its protruding eyes.

Ma Joong shrugged. 'So the murderer took the severed

head home. Well, I'd better climb up again. The constables will fetch ropes and a stretcher, and—Holy Heaven!'

A large block of masonry came hurtling down into the well, missing his left shoulder by the fraction of an inch. It landed on the back of the corpse with a thud. Quick as lightning, Ma Joong kicked his lantern over and, folding double, worked himself backwards into the niche. Putting his arms round his drawn-up legs and pressing his chin down on his knees, he just fitted into the hole.

Several pieces of masonry came plummeting down one after the other.

'Stop that, you fool!' he shouted. 'Ah . . . my shoulder. Stop . . .' He produced a series of agonized cries, followed by a loud howling that died out in low groans. More blocks of bricks came down, then a succession of mossy boulders. One bounced off the wall onto his left foot. With difficulty he suppressed a cry of pain. A few bricks fell into the well. Then everything was quiet again.

Ma Joong stayed in his cramped position as long as he could bear it, listening intently. When all remained quiet, he crept out of his shelter. Massaging his stiff legs, he stared up at the mouth of the well. When he was sure nothing was there, he retrieved his lantern and lit it.

Seng-san's body was buried under a heap of stones several feet high.

'We shall have quite a job delivering you of that burden later on, Seng-san,' he muttered. 'Right now, however, it'll give me a start up to the mouth of the well. And then I'll have a good look around for the well-wisher who dumped that load on you.'

87

X

Judge Dee looked down intently on Seng-san's headless body, which had been laid out on the trestle table in the mortuary. The judge was dressed in his nightrobe, his hair bound up with a piece of cloth. Ma Joong, his clothes mud-stained and torn, stood on the other side of the table, holding a large candlestick.

It was an hour after midnight. The Abbess had left as soon as the dinner was over. Afterwards the judge had played several games of dominoes with his three wives, then he had retired with his First Lady. In her bedroom they had drunk a few cups of tea, talking leisurely about their twenty years of married life, then they had gone to sleep. He had been awakened by the insistent knocking of the housemaster, who had informed the chambermaid in attendance that Ma Joong had arrived with an urgent message. Ma Joong had taken the judge to the mortuary at once, and reported on how he had made his discovery.

After a long silence, Judge Dee looked up.

'So that's why Seng-san's head didn't show the symptoms of strangulation,' he remarked. 'He was killed by a knife-thrust in his back. It was the other victim who was strangled. Have you any idea how your prospective murderer followed you, Ma Joong?'

'Our headman, the stupid ass, failed to tell young Fang

and the other constable about the second approach to the temple, from the rear. And I am just as stupid,' he added bitterly, 'for I ought to have looked behind the wall before going down into the well. There's a gap in the wall, and from there the scoundrel must have been following my movements. He probably was in the main hall when I came in, for I think I heard the small back door by the altar table close; but of that I am not sure. While the constables were busy hauling the body up out of the well, I inspected the rear of the temple compound and found that there's a path along the outside of the garden wall. The murderer must have walked along that path to the gap. He can't have followed me through the garden, for then I would have spotted him. Of that I am absolutely sure.'

'You also mentioned having seen a white shape.'

'Well,' Ma Joong said, a little self-consciously, 'that must have been a trick of the moonlight after all, sir. Spooks don't throw blocks of masonry about!'

Bending over the corpse, Judge Dee studied the intricate tattooing.

'The back is badly bruised by the bricks your assailant threw down the well,' he said. 'Seng-san was evidently a very superstitious man, like most of his ilk. Below the tiger mask he had a pair of mandarin ducks tattooed, the symbol of constancy in love. Under the one he put his own name, under the other—Heavens, hold the light nearer, Ma Joong!' The judge pointed at a smaller blue design that ran across the small of the back. 'Look! That's the profile of the deserted temple! Pity that the skin is torn by a brick. But I can still make out the four characters tattooed underneath: "much gold and much happiness".'

Judge Dee righted himself.

'Now we know why the murderer had to switch the corpses, Ma Joong! The motive of the crime was tattooed on Seng-san's back! Seng-san was after gold hidden in the temple. And the murderer too.'

'I questioned a fellow down town tonight who said he thought that Seng-san was blackmailing someone, sir.' Ma Joong outlined his theory about incriminating papers being hidden in the temple, and wound up: 'In that case, "gold" would not refer to a hidden treasure but to the money Seng-san was hoping to extort from his victim.'

'That's a possibility we must certainly keep in mind. It's a complicated case, Ma Joong! But at least we can eliminate the theory that a foreign barbarian was concerned in the murder. For we know now that Seng-san was killed by a knife-thrust in his back, and that the other man was strangled. To sever their heads after they were dead did not require any special skill in handling that Tartar axe.' The judge thought for a while, then added: 'Curious that the murderer didn't throw the severed head of the other victim into the well too. There was only a bundle of clothes, you say?'

'Yes sir. I put it over there, in the corner.'

'Good. We shall take those clothes to my study. Lock this door behind you, Ma Joong.'

Their footsteps sounded hollowly in the deserted corridor of the chancery. While they were walking along the judge asked, 'Who knows about your discovery of the body, Ma Joong?'

'Nobody but Fang and the other constable, sir. I explained to them that no one in the tribunal must know about my find. We carried the body here wrapped up in a blanket, and I told the guards it was the remains of a vagabond we found in the woods.'

'Very good. And the longer the murderer thinks he

did indeed kill you the better. Tomorrow very early you and Fang had better cremate Seng-san's body, together with his severed head. He apparently was a mean scoundrel, but he's entitled to enter the other world a whole man.'

Once in his private office, Judge Dee sat down heavily in his arm chair. His lieutenant lit the candle on the desk from the one he was carrying and sat down too. 'By the way, sir,' he said, 'when I entered the temple hall tonight, there was an awful smell there that reminded me of the stench of decay in the house of that dreadful woman Tala.'

'I didn't notice it when I was in the temple this afternoon. Must have been a dead bat; the place is swarming with them. Now that you mention the sorceress: when we were having dinner, the headman came to report that Tala has either left or gone into hiding, just as I feared. The constables searched the neighbourhood in vain. The people there were most co-operative, apparently they fear and hate her, and would be glad if we arrested the woman. You know how it is with those barbarians. As long as their sorcerers are successful, they venerate them like gods. But as soon as they fail, they show them no mercy. The Tartars there would like to kill Tala, if they dared. See whether there's some hot tea left in the tea-basket, will you?'

While Ma Joong was pouring the tea, Judge Dee went on, 'During dinner the Abbess told me that her maid is a flirtatious wench who makes up to the vagabonds that visit the temple. You might go there and make her talk a bit, Ma Joong. But don't let the Abbess know, for she said she wanted to be there when the girl was questioned. But in the presence of the Abbess the girl won't say a word, of course.' He set his cup down and suppressed a yawn. 'Well, let's now have a look at those clothes.'

Ma Joong opened the bundle. He draped a neat blue jacket and a pair of trousers over the back of his chair, and felt the sleeves. Then he also went over the seams. 'Not a thing, sir! The murderer took no chances.'

Judge Dee had been staring at the clothes, slowly tugging at his whiskers. Suddenly he looked up. 'You told me that Lee was looking for his assistant Yang who has disappeared. And the tailor told you that Yang associates with hoodlums and is a good-for-nothing. Ah-liu, on the other hand, informed us that Seng-san was working on some secret plan with a tall man, neatly dressed in blue, looking like a shop clerk. It's a long shot, of course, but isn't it possible that our unknown victim is no one else but that elusive painter's assistant?'

'Well,' Ma Joong said slowly, 'we might summon Lee Ko tomorrow and show him the corpse. Those painters have sharp eyes; he might recognize the shape of the hands, or the general stature and—'

Judge Dee raised his hand. 'No, I prefer to keep Lee out of this, as long as the matter of the ebony box hasn't been clarified. Fill the basin on the wall table over there to the rim with clean water, Ma Joong!'

When his astonished lieutenant had done so, Judge Dee said, 'Put it down here in front of me. Good. Now take that jacket and beat it with my ruler, over the basin!'

While Ma Joong set to work, the judge drew the candle closer and looked intently at the dust descending into the water. After a while he raised his hand. 'That'll do. Now for the trousers!' After Ma Joong had beaten those vigorously with the long wooden ruler, the judge said, 'All right. Let's see what we have got!'

He bent his head over the basin and examined the water closely. 'Yes,' he said with satisfaction as he righted

92

himself. 'It was indeed Yang! Look, those grey patches floating on the surface are common housedust. But do you see those very small particles that have sunk down to the bottom? Round the two on the right a diminutive red cloud is developing in the water, and there, where I point with my finger, you can see a yellow tinge, mixed with blue. Those are particles of powdered painter's colours. Yang must have got them in his clothes when cleaning up the mess on the table in Lee's atelier. We are making progress, Ma Joong!'

He rose and began to pace the floor. All his drowsiness had left him. Ma Joong tilted the water-basin with a happy grin. More small coloured clouds developed in the water.

The judge halted. Folding his arms in his sleeves he resumed, 'Now that one long shot has gone home, Ma Joong, I'll make another one. About the motive of the double murder. I don't think the blackmail theory will hold, at least not in exactly the way you meant. If, however, we take the word "gold" tattooed on Seng-san's back literally, it evidently refers to a hoard of gold hidden in the temple. Now Sergeant Hoong has studied all records relating to the temple's history with painstaking care, but he failed to find even a hint at a treasure having been buried there in the course of its long history. And even if there had been a hidden treasure, the constables would have discovered it when the authorities had the temple vacated. Trust them to have interrogated the inmates, and to have gone over the grounds with a fine tooth comb!'

He sat down again.

'My long shot is, Ma Joong, that they were after the gold of the Imperial Treasurer. Fifty heavy gold bars.'

'But that theft dates from last year, sir!'

D*

'Precisely. However, the thief had to lie low for a long time, waiting till the authorities had given up looking for the gold. Suppose he only told his accomplices, or his principal, that he had hidden it somewhere in the temple, without disclosing exactly where? And that the thief died before they had retrieved the treasure? Then the others would be in a quandary. They would have to search the temple and the entire extensive grounds. Yang and Seng-san, separately or together, caught them at it. First they tried to blackmail them—that's where your theory comes in, Ma Joong. But Yang and Seng-san had under-estimated their opponents, and were murdered.'

Ma Joong nodded eagerly. 'I think you've hit the nail on the head, sir! You can pack fifty gold bars in many different ways: in a large square package, in a flat or oblong one, in several small parcels, and so on. That would explain why the searchers looked both under the floors of the cells and behind the wainscoting in the towers.'

'Quite true. And the gold is still there, Ma Joong! For if the murderer or murderers or Yang and Seng-san had found it, then there would have been no sense in the switching of the corpses. They would have fled with the gold immediately after the murder; there would have been no need to prevent us from finding the tattooed clue. Nor would they have come back to the temple tonight, and tried to murder you. The gold is still in the temple somewhere, and we have to find it! We shall go to the temple tomorrow morning, Ma Joong. And now to bed!'

XI

The next morning at dawn, Ma Joong and the young constable called Fang burned Seng-san's body and head in the brick oven behind the prison. Afterwards Ma Joong had breakfast with Sergeant Hoong in the guardroom, giving the sergeant a circumstantial account of his adventure on the preceding night. Then they went together to Judge Dee's private office.

The judge briefly repeated his conclusions for the benefit of Sergeant Hoong. 'So we have now a double task before us,' he wound up. 'To discover the hidden gold, and to catch the murderer. This morning we shall proceed to the deserted temple with—Yes, come in!'

The headman entered. After he had wished the judge a good morning he said, 'The retired prefect, the honourable Mr Woo, wants to see Your Honour on an urgent matter. He is accompanied by Mr Lee Mai, the banker.'

'Ex-prefect Woo?' Judge Dee asked crossly. 'Oh yes, I remember. Met him once or twice at official functions here. A very lean man, with a slight stoop?' As the headman nodded, the judge went on: 'Quite a dignified, elderly gentleman. He was a diligent and scrupulously honest official, but his career came to an untimely end through an unfortunate affair. His uncle went bankrupt and Woo insisted on paying all the debts, although he was not bound in law to do so, of course. It nearly ruined him, for, since the uncle died soon afterwards, Woo never got a single copper back. He tendered his resignation, left his native city and settled down here, because the standard of life is much lower here than in one of the larger cities, and there are fewer social obligations. Who is that other man? Lee Mai, you said?'

'Yes, Your Honour. Mr Lee Mai owns a small gold- and silver-shop in the east quarter, and he conducts some banking business there also. He is a friend of the Honourable Woo.'

'Lee Mai's the brother of Lee Ko the painter, sir,' Ma Joong put in.

Judge Dee rose with a sigh. 'Well, go and receive our guests, Sergeant. Bring them to the reception hall. In the meantime I'll change.'

Ma Joong helped the judge to don his official robe of green brocade. A retired prefect had to be received with the honours due to his rank. While putting on his winged cap, the judge said with a bleak smile, 'Woo's visit comes at a most inopportune moment, but as an experienced official he'll at least state his case clearly and concisely!'

As the judge crossed the central courtyard with Ma Joong, he looked up at the sky. The heat was less oppressive than the day before; it promised to become a fairly cool day. They ascended the broad marble staircase that led up to the main entrance of the reception hall, built on a raised platform. Sergeant Hoong stood waiting for them between the red-lacquered pillars, and he led Judge Dee inside.

The two men seated at the tea table rose hurriedly when they saw the judge enter. The elder one came forward and made his bow. He had a long, sallow face

96

adorned by a wispy goatee and a long grey moustache, and was clad in a long dark-blue gown with a flower pattern embroidered in gold thread; he wore a high square cap of black gauze with a green jade ornament in front. While the judge made the prescribed polite inquiries of the retired prefect, he covertly observed the tall, broad-shouldered man who stood behind him. He had a pale, round face with heavy-lidded eyes, a short jet-black moustache and a diminutive chin-beard. He wore the grey gown and small cap of a merchant.

The judge bade the prefect resume his seat. He himself sat down opposite the distinguished guest. The banker remained standing behind the prefect's chair. Ma Joong and the sergeant sat down on low stools, somewhat apart.

After a clerk had served tea, Judge Dee settled back into his chair and asked, jovially, 'Well, esteemed colleague, what can I do for you, so early in the morning?'

The old gentleman fixed him with a sombre stare. 'I came to ask what news there is about my daughter, sir.' Seeing Judge Dee's uncomprehending expression, he added impatiently: 'Since you issued that proclamation last night, you must have news about Jade.'

Judge Dee sat up. He poured his guest another cup of tea. 'Before we continue this conversation, sir, may I ask why Mr Lee is accompanying you?'

'Of course. One month before my daughter's disappearance, I had promised her in marriage to Mr Lee. He has not married since, and therefore he has a right to know.'

'I see.' Judge Dee took a fan from his sleeve and began to fan himself. After some time, he said, 'All of this happened last year, before my arrival here. Since my information is mainly based on hearsay, I would greatly appreciate it if you would tell me briefly the circumstances of your daughter's disappearance. I failed to discover any concrete data in the archives here, you know.'

The old prefect frowned. Stroking his goatee with his thin hand he said, 'Jade is my only child, by my first wife who died three years ago. She is a rather clever but very headstrong girl. When she was getting on for eighteen, I selected Mr Lee Mai here as her future husband. I may add that Mr Lee had been assisting me in some financial matters, and I have found him a straight and well-educated man. Also, we are natives of the same district up north. My daughter approved of my choice. Unfortunately, however, I had engaged as secretary a young student called Yang Mou-te. He is a local man, well-behaved, and he came with good introductions. Alas, my advancing years are evidently blurring my powers of judgement. Yang turned out to be a scoundrel. Behind my back he made advances to my daughter.'

The banker bent and started to say something to the prefect, but the old gentleman shook his head vigorously.

'Hold your peace, Lee. Let me tell this in my own way! My daughter is ignorant of the ways of the world, and Yang succeeded in winning her affection. On the night of the tenth day of the ninth month, I told her after the evening rice that the following day I would consult a diviner about an auspicious day for her wedding to Mr Lee. Imagine my shocked astonishment when she coolly told me she would not marry Lee because she was in love with my secretary Yang! I had the scoundrel summoned at once, but he had gone out, and I spoke harshly to my daughter, very harshly, I admit. Who wouldn't, when confronted with such an outrageous affair? She jumped up and ran away.'

The prefect took a sip from his tea, shaking his head.

'Then I made a big mistake, sir. I assumed that Jade had run to her aunt, an old lady who lives in the street behind ours. She is a sister of my first wife, and Jade liked her very much. I thought that my daughter had gone to seek consolation there, and would be back the next morning, to apologize to me. When, at noon, she had not yet returned, I sent my housemaster to fetch her. He was told that Jade hadn't been there at all. I summoned Yang, but that rascal disclaimed all knowledge of her disappearance, and also brazenly stated that he had never exchanged more than a casual remark with her. I called him a liar, and had inquiries made. Yang had indeed passed the evening in a house of assignation. I dismissed the fellow anyway, of course. Then I called Mr Lee, and we made the most exhaustive inquiries, sparing no costs. But Jade had disappeared without leaving a trace. The logical conclusion was that she had been kidnapped when on her way to her aunt.'

'Why didn't you report this immediately to the tribunal, sir?' Judge Dee asked. 'In the case of a missing person, the authorities can take a number of effective routine measures and—'

'In the first place,' Woo interrupted, 'your predecessor was an ass, sir. And a coward to boot, for he didn't dare to lift a finger against Chien Mow, that abominable renegade who usurped power here.' He angrily tugged at his goatee. 'Second, I am an old-fashioned man, sir. The honour of my family means a great deal to me. I didn't want the fact that my daughter had been kidnapped to become public knowledge. Mr Lee entirely concurred with that view.'

'I plan to marry her, Your Honour,' the tall man said quietly. 'Regardless of what may have happened to her.'

99

'I appreciate your loyalty, Mr Lee,' the judge said dryly. 'But you gave Mr Woo wrong advice. The only correct course would have been to report the disappearance, and at once.'

The ex-prefect brushed the remark aside with an impatient gesture.

'Now, what did you learn about my daughter, sir? Is she still alive?'

Judge Dee put the fan back into his sleeve, and took from it a sheaf of papers. He leafed through them till he found his notes concerning Ma Joong's visit to the sorceress. Looking up, he asked, 'Was your daughter born on the fourth day of the fifth month, of the year of the Mouse?'

'Certainly, sir. You can find that in the records here in your chancery.'

'Exactly. Well, to my regret I can only tell you that the information I received regarding your daughter is very vague. At the present stage I could tell you nothing without running the risk of either unduly distressing you, or causing you to entertain hopes that may prove false. That's all I can say at this moment.'

'You'll handle the case as you see fit, sir,' Woo said stiffly. 'I have, however, one humble request to make of you. If your investigation reaches the stage that you feel compelled to take legal action, I'd be most grateful if you'd kindly appraise me in advance of the evidence.'

Judge Dee sipped his tea. He was wondering what his guest meant. The request seemed perfectly superfluous. Putting his cup down he said, 'I would've done so as a matter of course, sir. I—'

The prefect rose abruptly.

'Thank you, sir. Come along, Lee!'

The judge had risen also. Conducting his guests to the door, he said to the banker, 'I hear you have a brother who is quite a good painter, Mr Lee.'

'I know next to nothing about fine art, Excellency,' Lee replied, rather curtly.

Sergeant Hoong led the visitors downstairs.

'So that girl Jade exists, after all!' Ma Joong burst out excitedly. 'The sorceress must have known her, for the date of birth which she gave me was correct! That last message from her we found in the ebony box must be perfectly genuine, sir! Good Heavens, we must at once—'

'Not so fast, Ma Joong!' Judge Dee pushed his heavy cap back and wiped his moist forehead. 'I perceive strange undercurrents. It would not have been polite to press the prefect for details, but . . . What is it now, house-master?' He looked astonished at the greybeard who came shuffling inside, his thin face rather upset.

'Something quite unusual occurred in the women's quarters, sir. The First Lady sent me.'

'Well, speak up, man!'

'Just now the Third Lady came to see her ladyship, bringing a sealed envelope. She reported that a veiled woman came to the back door, in a closed sedan chair. Having inquired from the maids who was the youngest mistress, and having learned it was the Third Lady, she requested an interview with her, on a personal matter. When the maid asked her name, she handed over that sealed envelope. The First Lady opened the envelope, and found the visiting-card of Mrs Woo, the wife of the retired prefect. Her ladyship sent me here at once to ask for Your Honour's instructions.'

Judge Dee raised his eyebrows. 'I don't like my ladies to get mixed up in a case I am dealing with,' he told Ma

Joong with a worried frown. 'On the other hand, I have a distinct feeling that Mr Woo wasn't telling me the full story. Well, I shall take counsel with my First Lady. Tell the sergeant that we shall meet later, in my office.'

XII

Judge Dee found his First and Third Ladies in the former's boudoir. He told them briefly about the interview with the old prefect. 'Mrs Woo's visit must have a bearing on Miss Jade's disappearance. I would like to receive her personally, but she won't talk to me, of course. I ought to see her, though, to get an impression of her personality. . . .' He tugged vexedly at his sidewhiskers.

The First Lady turned quickly to the Third and asked, 'Can't you receive Mrs Woo somewhere in your apartment where our husband can see and hear her without his presence becoming known?' In accordance with the time-honoured custom, Judge Dee had assigned to each of his three wives a separate apartment, complete with their own kitchen and their own personal maids. Although the Second and Third freely went in and out of the First Lady's apartment in the main building of the residence, the latter never set foot in theirs. Judge Dee strictly adhered to this old-established custom because he knew that it offered the best guarantee for a peaceful and harmonious household.

'Well,' the Third told him slowly, 'as you know, the moon-door that separates my bedroom from the sitting-room has a curtain of thin gauze. If I make my guest sit down near the window, and you stood in the bedroom, behind the curtain, then—'

'That'll do fine!' the judge exclaimed. 'Let's go!'

'If you don't mind,' the Third Lady said, 'I shall take you there by the back door, so that the maids don't see you. They might tell Mrs Woo inadvertently that you are with me.'

'Excellent idea,' the First Lady approved. 'Good luck!'

The Third took the judge outside and along the winding garden path leading to her apartment, situated in a secluded corner at the back of the residence. As she was opening the door of her sitting-room to let him inside he said quickly, 'Try to make her talk a bit about Miss Jade. She's Woo's second wife, you know.'

'All this is very exciting!' she whispered, squeezing his hand. 'Look, I'll make her take that chair, facing the moon-door!'

The judge went on into the bedroom, carefully adjusting the gauze curtain behind him. It was half-dark there, for the shutters had been closed to keep the heat out. Sitting down on the edge of the broad bedstead, he heard his wife clap her hands. She told the maid that she could leave as soon as she had ushered the lady guest in, for she would look after the tea herself.

Judge Dee nodded approvingly. She was a clever woman. And of exquisite taste. He looked with appreciation at the graceful flower-arrangement on the tea table. Every time he came, he discovered something new. On the wall a poem she had written, or on the table a new painting done by her, or a piece of delicate embroidery. She was happy pursuing her own artistic interests and she loved teaching the children. Her father, an egotistic wicked man, had repudiated her after the terrible ordeal she had gone through in Peng-lai,* and the judge knew

* See Chapter XV of the novel *The Chinese Gold Murders*, London 1959.

104

she felt sheltered now, and considered his First and Second as her elder sisters. Voices in the sitting-room roused him from his thoughts.

The Third Lady was receiving a tall woman, sedately dressed in a grey robe with a long-sleeved jacket on top. It was fastened round the waist by a silk scarf, the ends of which trailed down to the floor. Her head was covered by a black shawl. As soon as the maid had left, the visitor unwound the shawl, tucked it away in her bosom, and made a bow, respectfully raising her hands folded in her sleeves.

'You'll have seen from my card who I am, madam.' She spoke in a clipped voice. 'A thousand thanks for kindly consenting to see me, despite the fact that I have not yet had the honour of being introduced to your lady-ship.'

Her mobile, expressive face was set off by a becoming high hairdress, without any ornaments. The judge thought she was not beautiful by classical standards; her lips were too full, her eyebrows a shade too heavy, and there were slight pouches under her large, vivid eyes. But she was certainly a woman of strong personality. He put her age at about thirty-five.

While guiding her guest to the chair near the window, the Third made the usual polite inquiries. Then she sat down and began to prepare the tea. Mrs Woo should have waited to open the conversation until the tea was ready. Instead, she began at once:

'I oughtn't to take too much of your time, madam, and I myself am in rather a hurry, for my husband mustn't know I am here. So please allow me to skip the formalities and come straight to the point.' As the Third inclined her shapely small head, Mrs Woo resumed quickly, 'My husband has gone to His Excellency this morning, to accuse me of having kidnapped his daughter Jade.'

The Third let a tea-cup drop onto the floor. It shattered on the marble slabs.

'I am so sorry!' Mrs Woo exclaimed contritely. 'How stupid of me to make such an abrupt statement! I should have told you the background first. Here, let me help you!'

After they had sat down again, Mrs Woo resumed at once. 'Of course I have never even dreamt of harming his daughter. I want to explain the situation to you, for as a young married woman, you'll understand. I hope that afterwards you'll kindly communicate the gist of our talk to your husband, so that he knows what's behind all this fuss.'

'I can't promise you anything before I have heard what it's all about, Mrs Woo,' the Third said in her soft, measured voice.

'Of course you can't!' Mrs Woo said impatiently. The polite veneer was rapidly wearing off. 'Let me begin by assuring you that I love my husband. He's twice my age, of course, but kind and considerate, and he gave me the security I wanted. Before my marriage I was what is called an abandoned woman, you know, and I hadn't a cent to my name. But that's neither here nor there. The main point is that when Woo married me he had been a widower for three years. He had only one child, a daughter called Jade. He thought the world of her, but I can tell you she was nothing special. Just an ordinary chit of eighteen, with men on her mind before she was quite ready for it. I wanted to take her in hand, but Woo said no, he would look after her education. He was fond of her, a bit too fond, if you know what I mean. Probably didn't realize it himself, but I have been around, and I knew. I didn't tell him that, of course, but I did tell him

THE THIRD LADY RECEIVES MRS WOO

that she was standing between him and me as man and wife, and that he'd better marry her off as quickly as possible. And that was the beginning of endless squabbles.'

She shrugged and went on: 'Now, husbands and wives will quarrel from time to time; that can't be helped. But when I smelled out that Jade had a boyfriend, I thought it my duty to warn my husband; and then the fat was in the fire! And even that was nothing compared with the row he made when the wench eloped with her lover. Woo shouted at me that I had murdered her, and hidden her dead body! After he had calmed down a bit, he realized he had been talking nonsense, of course. But then he developed the theory that I had had her kidnapped, to be sold to a brothel! I ask you!'

'Don't let your tea get cold,' the Third Lady said quietly, pushing the cup towards her guest. Mrs Woo gulped the tea down.

'Well, I denied that crazy accusation till I was blue in the face, but he wouldn't believe me. It so happened that I was away the night she vanished, you see. Had to see an old acquaintance.'

'Wouldn't it be the best proof of your innocence if you told your husband the name of his daughter's boyfriend, and where they went to?'

Judge Dee smiled. She was doing very well.

'If I'd known that, I would've told him at once!' Mrs Woo replied curtly. 'She made eyes at a Mr Yang, her father's secretary. But Yang is a decent young fellow, he feigned not to notice the wench. No, there must have been another man, but I never found out who it was. Her father gave her far too much freedom. Trust those modern young girls to handle their little affairs cleverly!'

'Well, couldn't you ask your friend to tell your husband you had been with him?' the Third Lady asked sweetly.

Mrs Woo shot her a suspicious glance. 'Well,' she replied slowly, 'to tell you the truth, Mr Yang had invited me. He's a man of the world, and he had noticed that my life was very dull. So he invited me for a bite in a place he knew. All above board, of course. But if my husband knew, he'd have a fit. He is a very fine man, but rather old-fashioned, you see.'

Mrs Woo heaved a sigh. Then she went on quickly: 'I shall be brief. This morning my husband suddenly told me he was going to take steps about Jade's disappearance. After nearly six whole months, mind you! Your husband the judge summoned him, I suppose?'

'That I really couldn't tell you, Mrs Woo. At home the judge never talks about official matters.'

'Wise man! Anyway, Woo had Lee Mai called. That's his best friend, a banker and gold-merchant. A bit pompous, but not a bad fellow. They rushed off to the tribunal together. Now I hope that you, having heard the whole story, will kindly suggest to His Excellency that he tells Woo it's in his own interest to forget all about his crazy suspicions of me. Then your husband can tackle the problem of the girl and her paramour. Your husband is a famous investigator, madam! He'll locate the couple before you can say knife! And that will settle this disgraceful affair for good. Then Woo'll treat me again as a husband should. He hasn't set a foot in my bedroom since that silly young bitch disappeared, believe it or not! Well, that's all.'

The Third Lady remained silent for a while. Then she said, 'I'll think over what you told me, Mrs Woo. But I must repeat that my husband dislikes discussing official

109

matters with his wives, and I doubt whether he . . .'

Mrs Woo rose. Tapping her lightly on her arm, she said with a smile, 'Any man will listen to a pretty young lady like you! Any man, dear! Thanks a thousand times for your kindness and your patience, madam!'

She wound the shawl round her head again. The Third Lady conducted her to the door.

When she had pulled the curtain of the moon-door aside, Judge Dee saw tears glistening in her eyes.

'It wasn't so exciting, after all,' she told him listlessly.

The judge pulled her down by his side and patted her hand.

XIII

The sergeant and Ma Joong had listened in astonished silence to Judge Dee's account of what Mrs Woo had said. The judge rearranged his notes and concluded: 'Mrs Woo is a vulgar woman, with a shrewd, intuitive insight into the carnal relations between the sexes, but who is wholly incapable of understanding the mentality of a man like her husband. Mr Woo wants to know what happened to his daughter, but at the same time he wants to protect his wife, regardless of what misdeeds she may have committed. That's why at the end of our interview he insisted on my promising I would acquaint him of the evidence at my disposal before taking legal action. For, should I discover that his wife was indeed concerned in his daughter's disappearance, Woo plans to persuade me to drop the case.'

'Do you think, sir, that there might be some substance to Mr Woo's suspicions?' Sergeant Hoong asked.

Judge Dee pensively stroked his moustache.

'I confess that I haven't the slightest idea,' he said at last. 'What I do know is that Mrs Woo's theory about Jade's eloping with a secret paramour is arrant nonsense. If Jade really had a lover, you may be sure that Mrs Woo would have ferreted out who he was! As to Mrs Woo's guilt. . . . She told my wife about her husband's sus-

111

picions with perfect candour, but that proves nothing, of course; she was firmly convinced that he had gone to me to accuse her. Mrs Woo is an extremely sensual woman, and protracted frustration often leads such women to excesses.'

'I can't understand,' Ma Joong spoke up, 'why the painter Lee Ko engaged Yang as his assistant after old Woo had kicked him out. And Yang was apparently gallivanting with Mrs Woo. We ought to know a lot more about Mr Yang. After all, he was the second victim of the murder in the temple!'

The judge had been glancing through his notes. Now he looked up and said slowly, 'It's a curious coincidence that Yang figures both in Jade's disappearance last year and in our present murder case. I don't like this affair. Not a bit! The fact that the sorceress Tala knew Jade suggests that there's a Tartar angle too.'

'I might consult Tulbee again and ask her to make inquiries among her people about a kidnapped Chinese girl,' Ma Joong said. He reflected that, compared with women like Tala and Mrs Woo, Tulbee wasn't so bad, after all.

'Yes, do that, Ma Joong. Perhaps Jade has been kept prisoner in some low den there in the Northern Row. First, however, you must get more data on Seng-san. If Miss Jade has really been kidnapped, we'll sooner or later get those scoundrels. But it is our urgent duty to find the temple murderer before he commits another outrage like the brazen attempt on your life last night.'

There was a knock on the door and a clerk came in.

'Mr Lee Mai the banker has come back here, Your Honour. He would be most grateful if Your Honour could see him for a moment.'

'Show him in!' To his two lieutenants the judge said,

'I noticed that Lee had something on his mind, but the prefect didn't let him speak.'

The banker seemed taken aback when he saw that the judge was not alone.

'Sit down, Mr Lee!' the judge told him impatiently. 'These two are my confidential advisers.'

Lee Mai took the chair Sergeant Hoong offered him. He carefully straightened his grey robe. Then, looking at the judge levelly with his hooded eyes, he said, 'I am most grateful that Your Honour grants me this interview. I couldn't speak freely in the presence of Mr Woo.' He cleared his throat. 'In the first place, I want to repeat that I consider Miss Jade still my fiancée, and that I shall marry her as soon as she has been traced, regardless of what happened to her during the past half year.' He resolutely closed his thin lips. Then he resumed: 'Second, I felt that Your Honour hesitated to tell Mr Woo the new evidence obtained by this tribunal because Your Honour didn't want to hurt him. Regarding me Your Honour doesn't need to have any such scruples. I am fully prepared to hear the truth, sir, no matter how distressing it might be.' He looked expectantly at the judge.

Judge Dee leaned back in his chair. 'I can only repeat, Mr Lee, what I said to Mr Woo earlier this morning.' As the other bowed resignedly, the judge went on: 'However, you would materially assist me in my investigation if you would tell me what measures you and Mr Woo took last year for tracing your fiancée.'

'With pleasure, sir. I went personally to the Chinese licensed quarter known as the Southern Row, and made discreet inquiries. When I obtained no result, I ordered my eldest clerk, who is a local man with a wide circle of acquaintances, to make inquiries in the underworld. He also drew a complete blank.' He cast a quick glance at the judge and resumed: 'I am convinced, sir, that Miss Jade was kidnapped not by local people but by a band of travelling touts, who took her away with them at once.' He rubbed his hand over his moist face. 'I have written to the masters of the Guilds of Gold and Silver Merchants in the five districts of this part of our Empire, enclosing traced copies of a portrait of my fiancée. But with no result.' He sighed. 'Your Honour was perfectly right in scolding me for not having urged Mr Woo to report to the tribunal at once. But it still isn't too late, sir! If you would issue a circular letter to the magistrates of—'

'I was planning to do that, Mr Lee. Could you let me have a dozen or so traced copies of Miss Jade's portrait?'

This question seemed to disturb the banker.

'Not . . . not right away, Your Honour. But I shall do my best to . . .'

'Good. Add a detailed description too. By the way, you might have those portraits copied by your brother. He, being a professional painter . . .'

The banker had grown pale. 'I have severed relations with him completely, Your Honour,' he said. 'I regret that I have to inform you that he is a man of loose morals. For many years he lived in my house, sponging on me. Didn't do a stroke of work. Just daubed at his paintings, or read strange books on alchemy or by heterodox philosophers. The nights he spent in gambling houses, taverns, or worse. He belonged to the same circle as Mrs Woo and . . .' He broke off and bit his lips.

'Mrs Woo?' the judge asked, astonished.

'I shouldn't have mentioned her, sir!' Lee said contritely. 'Now that I have done so, however, I may as well tell you, in the strictest confidence, of course, that I knew Mrs Woo and the man she lived with before her marriage to Mr Woo. The man was an able metal-worker who occasionally did odd jobs for me. But he was a crook and associated with crooks. When he left her, she came to me, asking whether I could help her to a job, perhaps in a shop. Woo happened to drop in, and he took a fancy to her at once. I wanted to warn him about the milieu she came from, but she swore to me that she had never taken part in any crooked business, and solemnly assured me that she would make Woo a good wife. I had to admit that she was a most energetic and capable woman, so I held my peace and Woo married her. On the fifteenth day of the fifth month last year, it was. I must say that she indeed managed his affairs very well. Unfortunately, she didn't get along with Miss Jade.'

'Yes, I heard rumours to that effect. Why?'

'Well, sir, Miss Jade was a sweet girl, with much book-learning but wholly ignorant of the ways of the world. Prone to look at things from a purely theoretical angle, you see. She made no allowances for the fact that her stepmother came from a quite different milieu but took an instant dislike to her. The dislike was mutual, I believe. Mr Woo understood and kept Jade's upbringing in his own hands. Quite an unusual situation, sir: a young woman having no elder woman to turn to for advice. Therefore I was overjoyed when Mr Woo proposed that I marry her. I am a bit older than she, of course, but Mr Woo said that Jade needed a husband who would have the patience to explain things to her and tell her what was going on in the world. In other words, a husband who could take the place by her side Woo himself had occupied since her mother's death.'

The banker smoothed his jet-black moustache with the tip of his forefinger before he resumed: 'I am deeply in love with Miss Jade, sir, and I think I may say that I am young for my years. My only hobby is hunting, and that keeps me fit.'

'Quite. By the way, do you agree with Mr Woo that his secretary Yang made eyes at Jade?'

'No, sir. I can't say I particularly liked Yang; he frequented the same establishments as my dissolute brother. But in the house his behaviour was always correct. He is a man of letters, after all.' He thought for a while, then went on, 'Perhaps Mr Woo was inclined to be a bit over-suspicious regarding the intentions of other men concerning his daughter. Miss Jade didn't have what you would call a happy home, sir, and that was one reason more why I wanted to have the wedding as soon as possible.'

'Thank you for your valuable information, Mr Lee. If there's nothing else you want to discuss, we'll now terminate our interview. I have several urgent matters to attend to before the session opens. I shall keep you informed about the progress of my inquiries.'

When the banker had made his bow and left, Ma Joong remarked, 'A decent fellow. We must try to . . .'

The judge wasn't listening to him. He said pensively, 'I wonder why Mr Lee came back here. Going over in my mind the gist of our conversation, I can only remember one question he asked. Namely, what new evidence I had found. He also made two specific statements: he reiterated his firm intention to marry Miss Jade, and he stressed the importance of looking for her in other districts. Hardly worth paying me a visit for! I find this very curious.'

'I think, sir,' Sergeant Hoong put in, 'that he also wanted to blacken Mrs Woo. His mentioning her name was no slip of the tongue. He brought up her past intentionally.'

'Yes, I had the same impression, Hoong. Well, let's

116

turn now to the double murder, my friends. I had planned to go to the deserted temple for a thorough search directly after breakfast, but all these visitors have left no time for that. We shall go there after the session. I shall close it as soon as possible—just make a few non-committal remarks about the murder in the temple and say that the investigation is still in progress and Ah-liu kept in confinement pending the results. You needn't be present in court, Ma Joong. I want you to look up that so-called King of the Beggars. Even though he doesn't wield much influence any more, he knows, of course, a lot about what is going on in town. Ask him whether he knew Seng-san. Then you might also try to find the man who tattooed Seng-san. There can't be many of them about, for the taste for that peculiar form of personal adornment is dying out. It's hard to believe, but touts and other low-class bullies are as fastidious about the dictates of fashion as famous courtesans! If you locate the fellow, ask him what comment Seng-san made when he had the profile of the temple tattooed on his back. I hope that . . .'

The headman came in, carrying two heavy dossiers. He deposited them on the desk and said, with an important air, 'Additional evidence has been forthcoming in the case Kao *vs* Lo, Your Honour. Kao is confident that, on the basis of this data, Your Honour will be able to settle the case during the morning session. I have brought the dossiers from the chancery, sir, for your inspection.' He dusted the covers of the dossiers with loving care. They contained all the documents relating to a most involved dispute about an inheritance that had been pending for several months, and which concerned large sums of money. Since it was customary that the winning party gave a generous bonus to the headman and his underlings, they took a deep interest in such cases.

'All right, headman. See to it that the courtroom is prepared for the session!'

As soon as the headman had closed the door behind him, Judge Dee exclaimed, annoyed, 'Of all the bad luck! I had entrusted the case Kao vs Lo entirely to our senior scribe. He has made a special study of it and has all the details at his fingertips! And now he is in Tong-kang! We shall have to go through those two files quickly, Hoong! The session opens in an hour! Take your time over those errands I told you about, Ma Joong. I greatly fear that the session will last till late in the afternoon!'

XIV

Ma Joong changed into the same old jacket and trousers he had worn when visiting Tulbee and Tala the day before. He went to the market and sat down at the long table of a cheap open-air eating-house, frequented by porters and chair coolies. He had a large bowl of spiced noodles, and then a second one, for they tasted very good. He belched contentedly, reached for a toothpick and said to the coolie who was gobbling his noodles beside him, 'That snake on your arm looks good. My wench told me I ought to have one tattooed on my breast, one that moves when I breathe. That'd tickle her no end, she says.'

The other surveyed Ma Joong's wide chest with an appraising eye.

'That'll cost you a lot of money! But you don't have to go far to spend it. The best man has a stall in the next passage.'

Ma Joong found the expert busily sorting out his bamboo needles. He watched him for a while, then told him in a surly voice, 'The tiger mask you put on the back of my friend Seng-san was no damn good! He was killed!'

'His own fault, brother! I told him that a tiger mask can't protect you properly if you don't have its red

119

whiskers added. That would've been ten coppers extra, because good red dye comes expensive, you see. Your friend refused. And see what happened to him!'

'He told me he didn't need any whiskers to his tiger mask, because the holy picture of the temple you tattooed across his hips was a powerful charm. Why spend ten good coppers for nothing?'

'So, it was a temple, was it? Seng-san said it was just a house, begging to be burglared! Much gold and much happiness, he told me to put underneath. Got neither, the poor bastard! What about you, mister? Want to see my book of samples?'

'Not me! I am a coward about pain! So long.'

He strolled on, pensively chewing on his toothpick. Seng-san had been close-lipped about the gold all right. When he arrived in front of the Temple of the War God, he went up the broad marble steps and bought two coppers' worth of incense sticks from the priest who sat dozing in his small office. Ma Joong lit the incense sticks and stuck them in the bronze burner on the altar. Above it rose the huge gilt statue of the deity, a fierce bearded warrior who brandished a sword ten feet long.

'Grant me a bit of luck today, will you, Excellency?' he muttered. 'And throw in a pretty little wench, if possible. There's an acute shortage of them in the cases I am now dealing with!'

In the street below a one-legged beggar stuck out his hand. Ma Joong put a copper in the dirty palm, and asked for the cellar of the King. The man gave him one look from his shifty eyes, sunk deep in the loose flesh of his face. Then he hobbled away on his crutches as fast as he could. Ma Joong cursed. He approached two loafers, but they only gave him a blank stare.

He walked aimlessly through the smelly alleys and

noisy back streets, trying to find a good place to ask about the elusive King's whereabouts. He knew that the poor are jealous of their secrets and, out of sheer necessity, always stick to one another. Tired and thirsty, he entered a small tavern. Sitting down at the greasy counter, he reflected that he would have to establish an identity. He was certain that nobody would doubt he was a vagrant ruffian; but they didn't know him, and that made all the difference. The half-dozen coolies at the counter eyed him suspiciously. Moodily staring at the liquor in the earthenware bowl before him, he again regretted that his colleague and blood-brother Chiao Tai wasn't with him. One carefully staged scene between the two of them would at once clear the hostile atmosphere.

When he had emptied his third bowl, the door-curtain was pulled aside and a slatternly woman entered. The coolies knew her; they greeted her with a few coarse jokes. One grabbed the sleeve of her faded gown. She pushed him away with an obscene curse.

'Hands off! I work only at night, the day is for sleeping. Had to see my old mother, she's spitting blood again, and no one to look after her. Give me a drink, I'll even pay cash!'

'Have it on me,' Ma Joong said gruffly.

'Why? Who are you?'

'From Tong-kang. A cousin of Seng-san.'

The coolies gave him an appraising look.

'Come to rake in his inheritance?' one asked with a sneer.

The others guffawed.

'I have come to settle the bill,' Ma Joong said softly. And when they suddenly fell silent, he added: 'Anyone want to help?'

'That bill is far too big for us, stranger,' an old coolie

said slowly. 'The thief-catchers got Ah-liu, and they'll chop his head off, naturally. But Ah-liu didn't do it. No one from among us. A damned outsider.'

'I don't care who it is, as long as I get my hands on him. What about the King?'

'The King is bad luck,' the prostitute muttered. 'Ask the girls who live there! Ten coppers a turn, sight unseen!' She gulped down her drink. 'Ask him, anyway. I seem to remember I once saw Seng-san about there.'

Ma Joong got up and paid their bill.

'Take me there,' he told the woman. 'There's ten coppers in it for you.'

'I'll show you the place gratis, for nothing. Seng-san was mean, but he was done in by a blooming outsider, and we can't take that.'

The coolies grunted their approval.

The woman took Ma Joong a few streets down. She halted on the corner of a crooked alley.

'At the other end is an old army barrack. The soldiers left; the wenches stayed. With their brats. The King lives in the cellar underneath. Good luck!'

The alley was paved with irregular cobblestones and lined by old houses built from large blocks of grey stone. Formerly well-to-do people lived there, but now every house was apparently inhabited by a dozen or more poor families. Every few steps Ma Joong had to duck to avoid walking into the pieces of wet laundry hanging on bamboos sticking out of the second-floor windows. Sitting on benches out in the street, the inhabitants were drinking tea and noisily discussing their affairs. Their wives hung out of the upper windows, listening and shouting down their advice. Farther along it grew more quiet. At the corner where the barrack stood there were but few passers-by. The wooden gate of the dilapidated building was closed, and no sound came from behind the shuttered windows. The women there were sleeping off the night before.

Beside the gate Ma Joong noticed a low, dark door opening. He stooped and looked inside. A steep flight of roughly-hewn stone steps went down into a cellar.

A dank smell of refuse greeted him when he slowly descended. The dark cellar was only about ten feet broad, but it seemed more than forty feet long, stretching out the whole length of the barrack's façade. The little light there was came from an arched window high up under the raftered ceiling, its base level with the street. And far back in the rear a spluttering candle stood on a low table made of logs. Except for a bamboo stool in front of the table, there wasn't a stick of furniture, and there seemed to be no one about. When Ma Joong walked on towards the candle he noticed that here and there water came trickling down from the stone wall, green with mould.

'Stay where you are, you!' a thin, reedy voice sounded above Ma Joong's head. He jumped aside and looked up. Against the iron bars of the window he vaguely saw a black bundle. Stepping up close, he saw that it was a small, incredibly old man who was sitting cross-legged in the corner of the arch. The completely bald, shining head, the long pointed nose and the scraggy neck coming out of the black rags made him closely resemble a vulture poised for swooping down on its prey. In his hands he held a long stick, ending in a wicked-looking iron hook. A pair of small, beady eyes squinted horribly at Ma Joong.

'Hold it!' he called out. 'I want to see the King. For a bit of business advice.'

'Let him pass, Cross-eye!' It was a deep, rumbling

voice from the rear of the cellar. 'Some people even pay for advice!'

The bird-like man in the window gestured with his stick that Ma Joong could go on. Footsteps sounded in the street outside. The small man peered through the bars with cocked head. Suddenly, with an incredibly swift movement, he brought the stick round, and stuck it outside through the iron bars. He hauled it back, plucked a mud-soiled piece of oil-cake from the hook and began to munch it contentedly. Ma Joong walked on to the table, thinking himself lucky not to have got the hook in his neck.

He strained his eyes but beyond the table he could discern only a pitch-dark vault, flanked by two heavy stone pillars. The one on the right seemed on the point of crumbling down, its outline showed large, uneven gaps covered with clusters of cobwebs.

'Sit down!' the deep voice spoke.

As Ma Joong took the bamboo stool, a huge, hairy hand appeared out of the dark and trimmed the candle with a thick thumb and forefinger. Now that the flame was burning high, Ma Joong found that what he had taken for a heap of crumbling masonry was in fact the formless shape of a bearded giant. He was sitting behind the table, hunched up on the raised base of the pillar. His broad, bent back fitted exactly into the cavity formed by the missing bricks. His tousled grey head was bare; long untidy locks hung down over his high, deeply grooved forehead. From under ragged eyebrows large slate-coloured eyes fixed Ma Joong with an unwavering stare. He wore a patched jacket that had faded to the indeterminate grey colour of dust.

'I am Shao-pa,' Ma Joong told him gruffly. 'From Tong-kang. A cousin of Seng-san.'

124

'He lies, Monk!' the old man in the window screeched. 'Seng-san never said nothing about a cousin!'

'Lao-woo is doing time,' Ma Joong went on quickly. 'It's my duty to get the bastard who got Seng-san.'

'Why come to me, Shao-pa?'

'Because they say in Tong-kang that you are the boss here.'

'Was the boss!' Cross-eye shouted. He burst out in cackling laughter. The other reached down, took a broken brick from under the table and threw it at the old man. His laughter ended abruptly in a scream of pain. He began to hop up and down in the window like a frightened bird in its cage. The man whom he addressed as the Monk looked Ma Joong up and down.

'You have Seng-san's build,' he remarked. 'I don't know who killed Seng-san, but I do know what Seng-san was after.'

'A fat lot of use!' Ma Joong scoffed. 'The gold in the temple, of course. The blasted murderer'll tell me where he hid it all right. After I have got him!'

The other said nothing. He slowly rubbed the table top with his big hand. Geometrical figures had been cut into the wood, here and there marked with strange, complicated signs. Holding the candle up, the Monk peered at the maze of lines, his large head with the wild mass of grey hair bent. Then he looked up.

'No, I have drawn too many diagrams here; the pattern has become confused.' It struck Ma Joong that, although the man's voice was coarse, he used the language of an educated person. 'I can't tell you much, Shao-pa. Not much. But I can give you one piece of sound advice. Get the gold, and forget about the murderer.'

'I won't forget, but there's no harm in getting the gold first. How much do you want?'

'Two thirds, Shao-pa.'

'Are you crazy? Half. I have to split with Lao-woo, mind you!'

'Like you split with me, Monk!' the man in the window called out.

'Done.' The Monk groped in his tattered sleeve and put a small square of wood on the table; it was inscribed with letters of some foreign script. 'Go tonight to the Hermitage, Shao-pa. That's a small temple, near the big red one, on the hill outside the east gate. Anybody can tell you. Climb over the wall and knock four times on the door of the servant's quarters, a small brick building to the left of the gate. Show this marker to the maid. Spring Cloud, her name is.'

'Spring in her pants!' Cross-eye jeered. The Monk threw a stone at him but missed. As it clattered to the floor, the old man burst out again in his cackling laughter.

'The eyes are going bad on you too, Monk!' he shouted.

'Has she got the gold?' Ma Joong asked.

'Not yet, Shao-pa. But she's mighty near to finding it. Together you'll get it.'

'That being so, why don't you go yourself?'

''Cause he can't walk!' Cross-eye jeered. 'If I didn't get him his grub, he'd croak like a mangy dog! And they still call him the King!'

'I am a bit feeble on my legs,' the Monk grumbled. 'Rheumatism, you know, deep in my marrow. Back and legs grew crooked. But I can still ride a horse, and my head is all right. Make no mistake about that, Shao-pa!'

'What about Yang? Doesn't he get a share too?'

The other scratched in his long, straggling beard, all the time fixing Ma Joong with his strange, still eyes.

126

'So you know about Yang too, eh? Yang has disappeared. Better look sharp, Shao-pa! You might disappear too. I don't know who did your cousin in, but he knows his job. Go to the Hermitage tonight.'

'Stay with the wench up there!' Cross-eye shouted. 'Dirt cheap!'

The Monk half-rose, pushing himself up on his mast-like, muscular arms. Ma Joong saw that the hulking shape would top him by at least two inches. But the giant's back was bent and his immense shoulders were sagging at an unnatural angle.

The small man began to hop to and fro in the window, the black rags flapping about like wings.

'Sorry Monk! Sorry boss!' he bleated.

'Shut up, Cross-eye. And stay shut up,' the Monk growled as he let himself down again. And, to Ma Joong: 'Goodbye, Shao-pa.'

He leaned back against the pillar. His head sunk on his breast.

Ma Joong got up, waved a hand at the old man in the window, and went to the stairs.

He strolled back to the tribunal, whistling a cheerful tune. His expedition had taken the whole of the afternoon, now dusk was falling. But the time had been well spent! The Abbess had warned Judge Dee already that her maid associated with vagabonds, and now he had learned that the wench had been planted there as an agent of the King of the Beggars! He might have an interesting evening—in more than one respect!

When the two enormous lampions of red oil-paper that lit the gate of the Temple of the War God came in sight, he again went up the broad stairs and burned incense. Evidently the deity was well disposed towards him!

127

At the tribunal the headman informed him that the judge and Sergeant Hoong were in Judge Dee's library, talking to the painter Lee Ko. Ma Joong went quickly to his own quarters, washed and put on clean clothes.

XV

The old housemaster was lighting the lanterns that stood in a row along the front of the marble terrace. Through the open doors of the library Ma Joong saw the judge standing at the large centre table of carved ebony, his hands behind his back. Sergeant Hoong was helping the painter to unwrap a few rolled-up scroll paintings.

When Judge Dee saw Ma Joong on the terrace, he said to Lee, 'I regret that you haven't managed to do that painting of the border scene for me yet, Mr Lee. But I know that superior paper is indeed hard to come by in this distant provincial town. And I fully understand that you don't want to paint a picture where the atmosphere is so important unless you feel in exactly the right mood. I would like very much to see the three landscapes you did last year. They could be hung somewhere on the wall here, I suppose. Tell the housemaster to get us more candles, Hoong. In the meantime I shall take a stroll in the garden with my lieutenant, to enjoy the evening cool.'

He took Ma Joong to a rustic stone bench under a high acacia tree below the far end of the terrace.

'The session dragged on till late in the afternoon,' he told his lieutenant. 'I had to adjourn it, for the other party had also found new data! I have seldom dealt with such a complicated inheritance squabble! Just after I had changed and taken a bath, Lee Ko came to see me. Presently we shall have a longer talk with him. What did you learn down town?'

Ma Joong reported the results of his afternoon excursion in detail. Judge Dee was deeply interested in his conversation with the King of the Beggars, nicknamed the Monk. He made Ma Joong repeat it verbatim.

'You did very well indeed, Ma Joong! Now at last we are seeing this case from the inside, as it were! The identity of the murderer remains shrouded in mystery, but we are getting nearer to the Treasurer's gold! Go tonight to look for it with that maidservant, that's much better than that we go there with a troop of constables! Try also to make her talk a bit on the Monk. He seems a most unusual person.'

The judge brushed a few blossoms from his lap and rose. They went back to the library.

The room was brilliantly lit by four tall candlesticks. Lee Ko and Sergeant Hoong were standing in front of three large painted scrolls hanging from the upper shelf of Judge Dee's bookcase, the wooden rollers at the bottom touching the floor. The judge turned his armchair round and sat down, facing the pictures. He silently studied them, caressing his sidewhiskers.

'Yes,' the judge said, 'that ink-landscape in the middle I like very much indeed. The two others are perhaps painted with a more delicate touch, but the brushwork of the middle one has the careless abandon of our ancient masters. There's a tremendous distance there. If you hadn't put in that small island on the horizon, one wouldn't know where the sea ends and the sky begins.'

'You have a deep understanding of painting, sir,' Lee

130

said gratefully. 'I always aim at creating depth and distance, but I seldom succeed.'

'If we ever succeeded in reaching the utmost of what we are longing for,' the judge said dryly, 'there would be a sense of surfeit. Sit down and have a cup of tea, Mr Lee.'

The old housemaster had come in with the large tea-tray. After they had tasted the tea, Judge Dee resumed : 'You are a great artist, Mr Lee. You ought to marry, so that you can pass on your art to your sons, in due time.'

Lee smiled faintly. 'Married life would engender the surfeit you just spoke of, sir. It robs love of romance, and then the creative spirit vanishes.'

The judge shook his head emphatically. 'Marriage is the basic institution of our sacred social order, Mr Lee. If you could live for ever inside four walls, then you could perhaps pursue love without its logical consequences. Since, however, you are compelled to go out into the world, you have to adapt yourself to human society. Otherwise the result is frustration. An ancient writer compared man with a member of a four-in-hand team. Within the team, each horse has a large measure of freedom, going slower or faster, swerving to left or right, for the chariot will never leave the track. The horse that breaks loose from the team may enjoy its complete freedom—for a certain time. But when it has become tired and lonely, and wants to rejoin the team, it finds the road gone and it can never catch up with the chariot again.'

The painter had grown pale. His hand trembled when he picked up his tea-cup. There was an awkward pause. Then Lee looked up and asked, 'By the way, sir, how is that murder case in the temple progressing? Have you obtained sufficient evidence to convict the vagabond?'

131

'We are making satisfactory progress,' Judge Dee replied vaguely. 'Slow but sure, you know.' He took a sip from his tea, to indicate that the time had come for his guest to take his leave.

Lee Ko was about to rise, when suddenly he clapped his hand to his forehead. 'How stupid of me! I had planned to tell you at once, sir, and it nearly slipped my mind! After you left yesterday, I remembered that I have indeed seen that small ebony box you showed me.'

'Well well,' Judge Dee said, 'that's interesting! When and where did you get it, Mr Lee?'

'About half a year ago, sir, from an old beggar. He came to the house, and implored me to give him a few coppers for it. It was all covered with mud, so I didn't see the jade disc on the cover. He said he had picked it up on the wooded slope behind the deserted temple, near a rabbit hole. I was busy and my first reaction was to send him away. But he looked so wretched that I took the box and gave him five coppers. I threw it into a basket with other knick-knacks. Later, when the old curio-dealer from behind the Temple of Confucius came to buy an antique painting from me, I threw in the basket to get from him the round sum I demanded.'

'Thank you, Mr Lee. I am glad that now I know where my box came from. Many thanks for showing me your work. I shall keep those landscape scrolls for a few days, and let you know when I have made my choice. By the way, has your assistant Yang turned up?'

'No, sir, but he'll be back soon! I made inquiries down town and learned he is on a spree with two boon companions. And that costs money!'

'I see. I happened to meet his former employer, the retired prefect Woo. He said he had dismissed Yang because he was a dissolute youngster.'

132

The painter angrily tossed his head.

'Woo is an old stick, sir! Exactly like my brother. They haven't the slightest sympathy for men who don't conform in every detail to their vulgar, dry-as-dust view of life!'

'Well, it takes all kinds of people to make a world. The sergeant will see you to the gate, Mr Lee.'

'So that box was found near the deserted temple, sir!' Ma Joong exclaimed.

'Yes,' Judge Dee said slowly. 'Very curious. If Lee is speaking the truth, it would seem that Miss Jade's disappearance is also connected with the deserted temple. And if it was his intention to tell me a fancy tale, then why did he choose this particular one?' He slowly stroked his beard for a while. 'And who would have given him the false information that Yang is on a spree with two friends? Yang is dead!'

Ma Joong shrugged his broad shoulders. 'That's easily explained, sir. As I told you, I met Lee yesterday when he was checking the taverns. And you know what those innkeepers are: they always try to put off a man who inquires after another with a few general statements. They don't like to get mixed up in other people's troubles. They have enough of their own!'

'I shall think all this over, Ma Joong. You had better go to the Hermitage after nine tonight. By then the Abbess will have said her vespers and be asleep.'

The judge walked along the open corridor that led round the inner garden to the apartments of his First Lady. Through the open window came the sound of a two-stringed violin, punctuated by the sharp clicks of a wooden clapper.

Entering the dark sitting-room, he saw that a number

133

of people were gathered there. They were all turned towards the improvised stage in the rear: a booth about seven feet high, draped with gorgeous red brocade, with along the top a screen of thin white cloth, lit by the oil-lamp hanging behind it. Small, brightly-coloured figures were flitting across it. From the booth came the sing-song voice of a story-teller, accompanied by the animated music of the violin. Judge Dee tiptoed to a corner, behind the audience. This was the shadow-play show his First Lady had promised the children, in connection with her birthday feast the day before.

His three wives were sitting on a long bench directly in front of the stage, together with the children and their nurse. Behind them stood the servants. Even the scullery maids had been allowed inside the house on this special occasion. All were following the play with rapt attention.

Folding his arms, the judge watched the colourful display. The graceful puppets, cut from thin parchment and painted with transparent colours, were manipulated behind the screen by iron wires. Now the performer pressed them close to the screen so that one saw, hair-sharp, their expressive profiles, then he let them flutter away from the screen, creating the illusion that they dissolved into the distance.

As was customary on such occasions, the play was a medley of auspicious legends, where the Queen of the Western Paradise predominated. Now she was haranguing her fairy court, standing under the Paradise Tree on which grew the peaches of immortality, painted a brilliant red. Gesticulating with her long-sleeved arms, the Queen resembled a large, gaudy butterfly. Then the white monkey who wanted to steal the peaches made his appearance. The children clapped their hands and

134

shouted their delighted approval when the monkey started upon his weird pranks.

Real life, the judge thought, was indeed even more of a medley than this shadow-play. Events unexpectedly overlap; motives get blurred by unforseen developments; the most carefully built-up schemes miscarry through a prank of fate; clever schemes get entangled in the infinite multiplicity of human behaviour. Therefore it was a mistake to seek to interpret the facts on the basis of a supposed preconceived clear-cut plan drawn up by the murderer of the deserted temple. He had to reckon with a very broad margin of error, and of haphazard coincidence.

He nodded slowly. Viewed in this light, he thought he could make a guess at the reason why the ebony box had been found in the vicinity of the deserted temple. And then the points that had struck him as incongruous in Miss Jade's message would find a logical explanation too. By Heaven, if his guess was correct, then Lee Ko's telling him how he got the box would be the strangest freak of fate he had ever encountered!

A loud rattling of the wooden clapper announced the end of the first act. The judge quickly slipped outside.

XVI

Now that he was going to visit the deserted temple for the second time, Ma Joong thought he had better explore the approach from the rear. So he left the city by the north gate.

He found the path leading up the slope without difficulty. Half-way up, however, there were several side paths, and he had to retrace his steps a few times before he got on to the track that took him to a small clearing on top of the hill. He paused there a few moments, enjoying the view of the city with its many twinkling lights.

After he had entered the wood, he found Fang, the young constable, sitting on a tree trunk. He told Ma Joong that his colleague was watching the head of the staircase on the other side of the hill. When he had showed Ma Joong the footpath leading to the Hermitage, Fang went back to his post.

Soon Ma Joong saw the red-lacquered gate of the Hermitage. The surrounding wall was not too high, and, as far as he could see in the uncertain light, the tiles that topped it were new and solid. It would not be difficult to climb over the wall, but he decided to wait until the clouds obscuring the moon had drifted away; for a dislocated tile could make a loud noise in the quiet night. Poking about in the undergrowth, he collected half a

136

dozen boulders which he piled up against the wall, to the left of the gate. As soon as the moon appeared, he stepped onto the pile and pulled himself up on top of the wall. The roof of the servant's quarters was directly below him, just as the King had told him. He crept a little farther and jumped down lightly in the paved courtyard. After a brief glance at the lighted window of the Abbess's living quarters he tiptoed to the door of the small building, and softly knocked four times.

When nothing seemed to stir inside, he repeated his knocking, pressing his ear against the wood. Now he heard the faint sound of bare feet. The door opened and he quickly stepped into a small room, lit by a cheap candlestick on the bamboo side-table.

'Now, who might you be?' the girl whispered after she had softly closed the door. She wore a thin nightrobe and he got a fleeting impression of a round face and a mass of tousled hair. He took the marker from his sleeve. Pressing it into her small, warm hand, he said:

'My name is Shao-pa. I am Seng-san's cousin. The King sent me. He told me you are called Spring Cloud.'

She stepped up to the side-table and studied the marker by the light of the candle. Beside it stood a round metal mirror on a wooden stand; in front of it lay a broken comb. This was evidently her dressing-table. Ma Joong cast a quick glance at the scanty furniture. Against the side wall stood a simple plank bed covered by a worn reed-mat, in front was a rickety bamboo chair. On a shelf high up on the wall he saw a tea-basket, a brass water-basin and a small lantern. The smell of a cheap perfume hung in the close air.

'Small but cosy!' he remarked.

'Mind your own business!' She stooped and took a small, low-legged table from under the bed. Having placed

137

it on the bed-mat, she sat down cross-legged beside it and gestured Ma Joong to sit down on the other side. He stepped out of his boots and followed her example. The mat was still warm from her body. They sat facing each other silently, the small bed-table in between them.

He noticed with satisfaction that, now that she had pushed the locks away from her face, she looked very nice, exactly his type: a pretty round face with saucy eyes, dimpled cheeks and a coral-red, full mouth. When he glimpsed her firm, round bosom through the thin robe, he said a silent prayer of thanks to the God of War. Suddenly she smiled.

'You aren't so young, but you look better than most of father's friends, Shao-pa!'

'Well, well!' Ma Joong exclaimed. 'So you are the King's daughter! An honour to work with you, Princess! I am supposed to help you get the gold, you know. Tell me how your father came to know about that. Seng-san used to be rather close-lipped—when he was still with us.'

'Simple. Father taught Seng-san boxing, formerly. That's why Seng-san used to look him up from time to time. He promised father a slice of the loot too.'

'How much was Seng-san to get?'

'One third, Yang two-thirds. Stands to reason, for Yang had tipped your cousin off, you see. Yang didn't like to look for the gold all by himself, for the fellow who had the first claim on it was a very tough customer, they say. Yang was afraid of him. And with a good reason, too! Seeing that the bastard killed your cousin and spirited Yang away to Heaven knows where! After that I told father I wouldn't go to search the temple at night alone any more. Not me!'

'I'd like to meet the son of a dog who killed Seng-san! His brother Lao-woo is doing time in Tong-kang, so it's me who has to settle the account.'

'As for me, father told me to apply for this job with the old bitch here to keep an eye on the temple. I won't say nothing bad about your cousin, mind you, but father just thought Seng-san would bear a bit of watching, you see.'

'The King was dead right! What I don't get is why the scoundrel who put the gold in the temple didn't dig it up himself and clear out. Why let it lie about there till Seng-san and Yang barged in?'

She shrugged her round shoulders.

'Seems he hid it because he stole it somewhere, and hid it so well that he couldn't find it any more! And not for want of trying either! I have been over that whole blasted place, and I can tell you he really did some work there! Tore up the floors everywhere. I have been over my employer's quarters too, by the way.'

'Heavens, Princess, you wouldn't suspect a pious abbess, would you?'

'As long as I don't know who owns that gold, I am trusting nobody. And as to pious, the old bitch has a nasty streak in her, brother Shao. If she's in a bad temper, she takes it out of me with a thin piece of rattan. "Let down your trousers, bend for the Lord Buddha and pray for improvement of your character!" she says, and then she lets me have it, counting the strokes on the rosary in her left hand! That's piety for you, brother Shao!' She spat on the floor. 'Well, now that you are here, I don't mind having another look at the temple. I'll show you the lay-out.'

She pulled a piece of folded paper from under the bed-mat and smoothed it out.

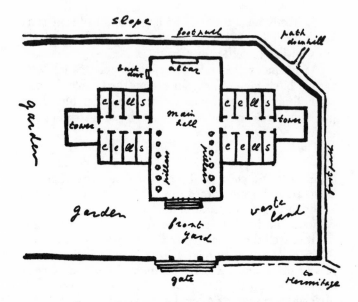

'Look here, this is the main hall, right in the middle. That's where we start.'

Ma Joong studied the floor-plan. It corresponded exactly to the description Judge Dee and Sergeant Hoong had given him.

'You did that very well indeed, Princess!'

'What do you think? I am an old hand at making floor-plans. Hire myself out as maid in a big house, and make a plan. Just so that a couple of father's friends don't get lost when they pay a visit there in the dark. You memorize this plan over by the candle there, brother Shao. We still have an hour or so, for we can't leave before the Abbess is asleep.'

Folding the paper up, Ma Joong said, with a grin, 'I'd like to use that hour to improve upon our acquaintance a

140

bit, Princess! Don't start on a job before you know your partner well, they say!'

'Business before pleasure,' she said determinedly. 'Get off the bed and study the floor-plan! In the meantime I'll change. Keep your back to me, and your eyes on that paper!'

Ma Joong stepped down and stood himself in front of the dressing-table, his back to the plank bed. She slipped out of her nightdress, and rummaged on her knees behind the bed until she had found a pair of dark-blue trousers and a jacket. About to put them on, she hesitated and gave Ma Joong's broad back a speculative look. With a faint smile she laid the clothes aside, knelt on the night-robe and began to do her hair. She thought that now she made a rather attractive picture, and called out, 'Don't turn round yet!'

'Why should I?' Ma Joong asked. 'I am doing fine with the mirror here. You looked very nice from behind, too!'

'You mean bastard!' She jumped from the bed and went for him, trying to scratch his face. He folded her in his arms.

When she had dressed she took the small lantern down from the shelf.

'We can light it only when we are inside the temple,' she said. 'This afternoon I saw a couple of fellows hanging about near the gate, and they looked like thief-catchers, posted there after your cousin's murder. So the fellow who did him in won't be around tonight. We might meet the ghost, though.'

'Don't try to be funny, Princess!'

'I don't. There is a ghost about there. Saw her a couple of times myself, with my own eyes. Floating about the trees, she was. A tall woman, in a creepy white shroud.

141

I don't like ghosts, but this one means no harm. Once I nearly bumped into her. She didn't do a thing, just looked at me with her large sad eyes and drifted on.'

'Sad or not, I don't like to meet her. Let's be on our way! I'll get you past those guards. I was in the "green woods" in my younger days.'

She blew out the candle and opened the door a crack.

'Funny!' she whispered. 'There's still a light in the old bitch's room!'

'She'll be reading her holy books!'

'And aloud too, by the sound of it. Well, we'll go anyway. If she discovers I am out, I'll give her notice. Let her pink another girl's behind!'

They crossed the yard on tiptoe. She carefully lifted the crossbar, opened the gate and put a few pebbles underneath so that it remained ajar. They walked down the path through the forest. Arrived at the edge, he told her to stay close behind him, and do exactly as he did. He studied the trees at the top of the staircase, trying to locate the constable on duty. It would be awkward if the man spotted them. Yes, there he was, the lazy dog! Asleep under that cypress tree! Well, it made things easier, anyway. About to drag Spring Cloud along, he suddenly stiffened. There was something strange about the man's drawn-up knees and his outflung arms. He quickly went over to the prostrate figure and bent over it.

'Is . . . is he dead?' she whispered behind him.

'Strangled from behind with a thin cord,' he muttered grimly. 'Go back home, Princess. From now on this is strictly a man's job. The murderer has come back.'

She clasped his arm.

'I'll stay with you. I have been in scraps before. If you come to grips with him, I can always bash his head in with a brick.'

142

A MEETING LATE AT NIGHT

'Have it your own way! The bastard is probably in the main hall, so we can't risk the front entrance. We'll take the back door, first climbing over the outer wall at the rear.'

'Yes, there's a gap just a little beyond the back wall of the hall. Come along, I'll show you!'

They walked along the front of the outer wall, turned the corner and then followed the path leading along the temple's side wall. When they had come to the small clearing at the north-east corner, Ma Joong halted.

'Wait here a moment,' he whispered. 'I'll reconnoitre.'

He went on to the tall trees, looking for the young constable. But, although he went as far as the clearing where the path led down the slope, there was no trace of Fang. He whistled, softly. All remained silent. He cursed under his breath. Had the murderer got Fang too? Suddenly he had the uncanny feeling that someone was watching him. A cloud was obscuring the moon again. He strained his eyes but nothing seemed to be moving under the high oak trees. He went back to where he had left Spring Cloud.

'There's nobody about,' he told her. 'You stay here, it's better that I have a squint at the rear wall first. I'll come and fetch you if the coast is clear, and then you can show me that gap where we can climb inside.'

He went round the corner, his left hand on the weather-beaten bricks of the outer wall. There was no one on the long narrow path that ran all along the back wall of the temple. On the right of the pathway was the steep slope down, covered with thick shrubs and here and there a large, mossy boulder.

Standing there at the corner he scanned the top of the wall. The bricks had crumbled away in several places, but he couldn't see the larger gap Spring Cloud had spoken

144

of. At the far end, beyond the silhouette of the west tower, he saw the pile of masonry that marked the opposite corner of the outer wall, where the old well was located. If necessary they could walk on to there, and then . . .'

He bent forward. In the shadows near that far corner he saw a white shape. Not trusting his eyes, he quickly advanced a few steps. Then he stood stock still. It was the white woman, beckoning him with a long, thin hand.

XVII

He stared at the apparition, spell-bound. Then it flashed through his mind that the other night the phantom had led him to the hidden path. Would she now . . . ? He raced down the path.

'Brother Shao, I . . .' Spring Cloud called out behind him. Suddenly the ghostly apparition raised her arms high above her head. The moonlight shone through her long, silvery sleeves. Ma Joong halted abruptly; he didn't know what to think of the menacing gesture. The girl bumped into his back. At that very same moment the upper part of the wall above him crashed down, directly before his feet.

For one brief moment he stood there motionless, staring dumbfounded at the mass of broken masonry that blocked the path.

'What happened . . .? What . . . ?' the girl gasped behind him.

'That was meant for us!' he hissed. 'Stay here!'

He quickly climbed on to the heap of bricks. From there he could grasp the rough edges of the gap higher up in the wall. He pulled himself up, climbed on the wall and jumped down into the back yard of the temple, just in time to see a black shape disappear through the back door of the main hall.

146

Ma Joong ran to the door, dropped on all fours, and quickly crept inside. He crouched with his back against the wall, just inside the door, on the right, ready to clasp the other's legs should he be waiting there. But nothing stirred in the darkness. He carefully explored the space within his reach but his groping hands met only emptiness. At the far end of the hall he saw a faint light. That must be the latticework of the six-fold entrance door. Again he noticed that awful, nauseating stench of the day before. The only sound he heard was the flapping of a frightened bat. Yet the murderer had to be there, somewhere in the dark hall. Here they would fight it out. He reflected with grim satisfaction that he had the advantage, even if the murderer should be armed. For Ma Joong had fought many a fight in pitch-dark places and he knew all the tricks. And, thanks to his previous visit and Spring Cloud's sketch, he had a clear picture of the situation.

With infinite care he crept along the wall, advancing inch by inch towards the left corner, his right shoulder brushing the stone surface, his muscles tense for quick action, his ears straining for a tell-tale sound.

Arrived in the corner, a piece of cloth suddenly grazed his groping left hand. He shot forward, stretching out his long arms to grab his opponent's legs. But there was nothing, and he bumped his head hard against the wall. Half-dazed, he heard the quick shuffle of feet, directly ahead. Then there was the clanking of iron on stone. That meant his opponent had a sword. He lay completely still for a while. Then he groped about, and understood what had happened. What he had taken for a piece of the other's robe proved to be nothing but a cluster of cobwebs, stiffened by dirt.

His head was reeling but he knew he had to get away

from that corner as fast as possible. The side door leading to the monks' cells couldn't be far away. After he had crept along the wall for some time, his fingers met the rough surface of wooden boards. Now on to the niche where the ritual arms were kept. Yes, he felt two thick shafts. The two halberds were still there. But apart from those the niche was empty. Now he knew his opponent's weapon: it was the second Tartar axe. He reflected with a wry grin that he was lucky. For an axe is of slight use in a fight in the dark, whereas a halberd is a wonderful weapon. He knew how to handle it: more than ten feet long, the point would penetrate a leather cuirass, the razor-sharp blade beneath the point would split a skull, and the wicked hook opposite could be used for pulling a knight from his horse, or for bringing a fleeing foot-soldier to the ground. And he had two, one for fighting, the other for reconnoitering and for setting a trap! He righted himself and took the halberds noise-lessly from the niche, holding their shafts upright. While he stood there motionless, waiting for the painful throb-bing in his head to subside, he tried to orientate himself. He was standing now by the last pillar of the row to the left of the entrance. On his left hand was the empty space in front of the altar. He levelled the halberd in his right hand and explored the floor space with it. When all proved to be clear there, he turned and verified that no one was in the narrow space between the row of pillars and the wall. Holding the two halberds upright, he tip-toed to the centre of the hall, and stood there facing the entrance.

The rectangle of the six latticework panels stood out clearly. Of course the other man would avoid the central part of the hall, between the two rows of pillars, for there he would be seen against the light of the lattice doors. He must be hiding in the space behind the row of pillars to the right of the entrance, now on Ma Joong's left. A slow grin spread over his face.

He went step by step to the left, till he had arrived by the last pillar. He went to stand squarely in front of it, and set up the halberd in his left hand against it. Then he took a firm grip with both hands on the other. Presently he would kick the standing weapon over, so that it would clatter down in the space behind the pillars. His opponent would come out and be clearly outlined against the lattice doors. Then he would get him with the halberd he still held.

All at once he held his breath. He thought he had heard a faint noise, on the other side of the pillar he was facing. Suddenly a large dark shape shot forward, knocked the halberd in his hands aside and made for the lattice door. Ma Joong lunged the halberd forward but he was too late, the fleeing shape was just out of reach. With a curse he let the halberd drop and ran after him. The dark shape halted in front of the door. A heavy object whizzed past Ma Joong's head and clattered to the floor behind him. Then the man kicked a panel open. Ma Joong threw himself forward to tackle him. His feet got caught in a rope on the floor and he fell flat on his face. After he had scrambled up he rushed through the open door out into the front yard, and got just a glimpse of something moving by the triple gate. When he had ran out there, he faintly heard the sound of feet on the staircase, far below. His opponent had escaped.

Cursing volubly, he wiped the blood from his face. A large lump was forming on his forehead. He went inside and retrieved the halberd. With vicious jabs he broke all the six panels down. Now he saw that the rope his feet had got entangled in was in fact a rope-ladder, made of thin, tough silk cords. At one end it was provided with two large iron hooks. Further down, at the foot of the last pillar, lay the Tartar axe the other had thrown at him.

He left the hall by the back gate. Spring Cloud sat on her haunches in the gap, clasping the lantern in her hands. He climbed up, kissed her tear-stained face, and helped her down on the other side.

'The son of a dog escaped, Princess! Did you see the ghost?'

'A ghost? No, I saw nothing. Was I in a blue funk? Hey, you look terrible! Here, let me wipe your face!'

'Don't bother. I'll deliver you to the Hermitage, then have a last look around for that blasted ghost.'

He put his arm round her shoulders and walked back with her to the Hermitage.

'You'll see more of me, Princess, one of these days!' he said. Pushing her inside, he cast a casual look at the quarters of the Abbess. The window was dark now.

He hitched up his trousers and went back to the clearing where he had seen Fang sitting on the tree trunk. He whistled shrilly on his fingers. The hooting of an owl was the only answer. With a worried frown he lit the lantern and began to search the undergrowth systematically, cursing savagely when the thorny branches tore at his trousers. He knew that Fang would never have gone far from his watchpost.

Struggling through a clump of wild roses, he came out in a clearing, in front of a group of high yew trees. As he started to cross it he stepped with his right foot into a hole and fell with his face on a round boulder.

'That's the third time tonight!' he muttered as he scrambled up. With a sigh he picked up the lantern and relit it with his tinder-box. Suddenly he gasped. What he had taken to be a moss-overgrown boulder was the mangled head of a man.

A sick feeling rising in his stomach, he let the light shine on the distorted face. Then he heaved a deep sigh of relief.

'Heaven be praised!' It wasn't Fang. The face was completely unknown to him.

He gave the hole a good look. It was newly-made, a small pile of wet earth was beside it. He gazed again at the grisly object at his feet.

'Holy Heaven, it must be Yang's head, buried here by the murderer! But why did he dig it up again?'

He raised the lantern and inspected the yew trees. A man was lying in the tall grass below, beside his head a crushed constable's helmet. With a smothered curse Ma Joong bent over the prone figure and felt his breast. Fang was still alive.

Ma Joong carefully turned the head of the unconscious man a little. There was a gaping wound at the back of his skull. He felt the area surrounding it, his fingertips delicately parting the matted hair.

'It was a nasty blow all right,' he muttered. 'But as far as I can see it didn't damage his skull. Those helmets are solidly made. There's an awful lot of blood, but that can't be helped in the case of a head wound.' He picked up the helmet. 'Yes, the foul bastard hit him with that Tartar axe. The helmet may have saved Fang's life, but there's no time to be lost. I must get the Abbess at once, and ransack her household pharmacy.'

He ran down the path to the Hermitage.

After he had rattled a brick on the gate for a considerable time, the peephole opened. Through the grating he saw the astonished face of Spring Cloud, and that of the Abbess behind her. He reached down and took his identification document from his boot. Holding it up in front of the peephole, he told the Abbess, 'I am Ma Joong, one of Judge Dee's lieutenants, Reverend Mother. I found in the wood a wounded man who needs immediate medical attention.'

'Open up!' the Abbess told the girl.

In the courtyard Ma Joong explained the situation to the Abbess.

She nodded gravely and said, 'Fortunately I have a well-equipped pharmacy here. Looking after the sick and wounded is part of our religious duties. The maid will take you to the kitchen. The bamboo screen there might well serve as a stretcher. She will help you to carry the wounded man here; she is a strong girl. I shall look after him. I shall now prepare a bed in the side-hall.'

As soon as they were in the kitchen, Spring Cloud turned on Ma Joong with blazing eyes.

'Liar!' she hissed at him.

Ma Joong didn't know what to say. The War God had left him in the lurch! They took the bamboo screen down in silence. She looked at him sideways, and said, suddenly, 'You are rather a nice liar, though.'

'Good!' said Ma Joong with a broad grin. 'You are magnanimous! A real Princess!'

Judge Dee was in his private office, going over the dossier regarding the financial administration of the district with Sergeant Hoong.

'Good Heavens, what happened to you?' the judge exclaimed when he saw the big lump on Ma Joong's forehead, and his torn and mud-covered clothes. 'Pour him a cup of hot tea, Sergeant!'

Ma Joong gratefully sipped the strong tea. Then he began his story. He concluded:

'The Abbess cleaned Fang's head wound expertly, sir. She's a remarkable woman, remained as cool as a cucumber all through. When we had put ointment on the wound and forced a drug down his throat, he regained consciousness. He said he had noticed that some digging had been done in the clearing recently. Just when he had discovered Yang's severed head, he was struck down from behind. The Abbess has given him a sedative, and when we left he was sleeping peacefully. The Abbess says that, if he doesn't develop a fever overnight, he'll pull through all right.' He emptied his seventh cup, and added, 'I haven't yet told the headman about the murder of the other constable, sir. How shall we break this bad news to the men?'

'Order the headman to assemble them in the guardhouse, Ma Joong. Then tell them on my behalf that I give them my word that the murderer shall get his deserts. Add that it is in their own interest that they keep this murder strictly secret. Then order the headman to go to the temple with a stretcher and fetch the dead body, and Yang's head.'

Ma Joong nodded and went out. Judge Dee silently stroked his beard for a while. Then he said to Sergeant Hoong:

'We lost a good man, and another was severely wounded. We have obtained two important clues, but the cost was high, Sergeant.'

He put his elbows on the table and stared with unseeing eyes at the financial documents before him, deep in thought. Suddenly he looked up and asked, 'Why is the murderer in such a terrible hurry all at once? For months on end he contented himself with patiently searching the temple. And now, in the brief space of two days, he first commits a double murder, then tries to kill

153

Ma Joong twice, murders one constable and attacks another! Why this sudden urgency?'

The sergeant shook his head, a worried expression on his thin face.

'For some reason or other the man has become desperate, sir. Attacking an Imperial officer is no small matter. Everybody knows that the authorities will never give up finding the perpetrator, and that he will be executed in the severest manner allowed by the law. That's why constables can go about their duties armed only with a club. If it's bruited about that someone had the audacity to attack a constable on duty, it might affect the safety of our entire personnel, sir.'

'Yes, I have thought of that aspect, Hoong. That's why I told Ma Joong to enjoin the constables' complete silence.'

The judge lapsed into sombre thought.

When Ma Joong came back, Judge Dee took hold of himself. Sitting up straight, he said briskly, 'The gold must be hidden in a high place, otherwise the murderer wouldn't have brought a rope ladder. Second, we know now that at least three parties are after the gold. Namely, the murderer who organized the theft, Yang and Seng-san who barged in, and the King of the Beggars who had been promised part of Seng-san's share. As I have just explained to the sergeant, there is one point that is exercising me considerably. I mean the sudden urgency on the part of the murderer. I wonder whether that could be explained by an entirely new personality having entered upon the scene, a man who has nothing to do with the theft of the gold. That idea, however, is based only on an intuitive feeling. Finally, the problem of the phantom. Until tonight I had dismissed the ghost as just a figment of the imagination of superstitious persons. Ma Joong

154

himself wasn't certain he had actually seen her yesterday. But tonight he has seen her clearly, and he saw her taking an active part in the murderous attack on him. So from now on we shall have to take full account of that mysterious apparition. What is your opinion, Ma Joong?'

Ma Joong gloomily shook his head.

'No matter what or who that spook is, sir, she is in league with the murderer. The other day she didn't point out the hidden path to the well in order to help me, as I foolishly thought. She did it just to lure me to that far corner of the garden, where the murderer was waiting for me behind the gap in the outer wall. When they saw me going down into the well, they thought that killing me there would save them the trouble of disposing of my dead body. Tonight that damned spook was encouraging me to walk on, drawing all my attention to herself, so that I wouldn't notice that the murderer was working loose the upper portion of the crumbling wall. But she made a bad mistake when she suddenly raised her arms as a sign for the murderer that I was in exactly the right spot. The gesture frightened me. I halted, and that saved my life—with not a fraction of an inch to spare!'

Judge Dee nodded. He consulted his notes, then he asked, 'Couldn't you give me a better description of the phantom?'

'Well, sir, both times I got only a glimpse of her and both times it was from quite a distance, and in the uncertain moonlight. She wore a robe of thin gauze, I think, and she had a piece of the same material wound round her head, covering her face. She was tall, of that I am certain.'

'Are you quite sure it was a woman, Ma Joong?'

Ma Joong pulled at his small moustache. He said, hesitating, 'Everybody spoke about a white woman . . . And that long robe . . . but that doesn't count, of

course, for a man can put on a long woman's robe too.
. . . Well, there's the figure, of course. Broad in the hips
and narrow in the shoulders. Did I see her bosom, now?
Yes . . . or . . . ?' He shook his head disconsolately.
'I am sorry, sir. I really don't know!'

'Don't worry, Ma Joong! The main thing is that we
now know it is an ordinary human being of flesh and
blood. Well, you must go to the Hermitage first thing
tomorrow, Ma Joong, and see how Fang is getting along.
We shall meet here again after breakfast. We must do
something, and very soon too. The murderer is desperate,
and he may strike again at any moment. Open the window, Hoong! It's getting so stuffy that I fear we may
be in for a rainstorm. And they can be very violent, this
time of the year. I'll remain here for a while, trying to
sort out my thoughts. Good night!'

XVIII

The violent rainstorm that had broken loose over Lan-
fang a few hours before dawn had cleared the air. When
Judge Dee, accompanied by his Third Lady, went into
the garden for an early-morning stroll, a cool, thin mist
was hovering over the pond where a profusion of pink
and white lotus flowers had suddenly opened. The judge
decided to have their morning-rice served in the water
pavilion.

They ate in silence, enjoying the fresh air and the
charming scenery. Afterwards they stood at the red-
lacquered balustrade, and fed the left-over rice grains to
the goldfish. Watching their swift moves as they came
dashing out from under the large leaves, the Third Lady
said :

'You came home very late last night, and you slept
badly, tossing about all the time. Was there bad news?'

'Yes. We lost a constable who leaves a wife and two
children, and another was severely wounded. But I believe
the end of this distressing case is in sight. Only one
last piece is still missing, and that I hope to discover
today.'

She went with him as far as the garden gate.

He found Ma Joong and Sergeant Hoong waiting for

him in his private office. After they had wished the judge a good morning, Ma Joong said:

'I have just come back from the Hermitage, sir. Fang is doing well. The Abbess thinks that, after ten days or so, he'll be perfectly all right. She offered to let him stay there till he has completely recovered.'

'That's good news!' the judge said, sitting down behind his desk. 'Yes, Fang had better remain in the Hermitage, for the time being. Well, last night I went over again the various aspects of our case. I decided that today we should first make a second search of the deserted temple, then have the King of the Beggars and his daughter in, for a thorough interrogation.'

Ma Joong shifted in his chair. He cleared his throat and said, 'To tell you the truth, sir, I got the impression that Spring Cloud sometimes acts as scout for her father's thieving beggars.'

'That is what I thought when I saw the floor-plan she made of the deserted temple,' Judge Dee remarked dryly. He opened his drawer and put the sheet of paper on his desk. Smoothing it out, he added: 'It's very useful for our orientation, I must say.'

Ma Joong got up. Bending over the desk, he said eagerly, 'On this plan I can trace for you exactly how I tried to catch the murderer last night, sir. Look, the gap through which I entered the compound is here. I slipped inside by this door and . . .'

He went on to describe the contest in the dark hall, step by step. Judge Dee listened absent-mindedly. He was tugging at his whiskers, staring fixedly at the plan.

'Then my feet got caught in that blasted rope-ladder,' Ma Joong went on. 'Here it was, right in this spot. So—'

Suddenly Judge Dee hit his fist on the table, so hard that it made the cups ring.

158

'Holy Heaven!' he exclaimed. 'So that is what it was! Why didn't I see that at once? During my visit to the temple I got a good idea of its layout, yet I failed to notice the close resemblance!'

'What . . .' Sergeant Hoong began.

The judge pushed his chair back and got up.

'Wait! I'll have to work this out logically. Thanks to that girl's skill, I have found the missing piece, my friends! Let me now see where exactly it must be fitted in. . . . Yes, at last a definite pattern is arising from all this confused data. But . . .'

He shook his head impatiently and began to pace the floor, his hands behind his back.

Ma Joong smiled contentedly. During his visit to the Hermitage he had found an opportunity for talking with Spring Cloud alone for a few minutes, and he thought she didn't seem averse to becoming his regular girlfriend. That she had apparently provided the judge with an important clue might make it easier to straighten out her former petty offences. There was a pleased look on Sergeant Hoong's face too, for he knew the signs from long experience: the case had arrived at a turning point.

Quick steps of heavy boots resounded in the corridor. The headman came bursting in.

'The warden of the north-west quarter came rushing here, sir!' he panted. 'There's big trouble there. The Tartars are stoning the sorceress to death. When the warden's men went to stop them, the scoundrels chased them away, pelting them with sticks and broken bricks. . . .'

Ma Joong gave the judge a questioning look. When Judge Dee nodded, he jumped up, pulled the heavy whip out of the headman's belt and ran out.

In the stable yard two grooms were rubbing down a

159

horse. Ma Joong sprang on its bare back and rode through the gate.

In the street he drove his horse to a gallop. The crowd made way hastily when they heard the clatter of the hoofs and saw the horseman approaching. The streets of the north-west quarter had an ominous deserted look. Over the low roofs ahead Ma Joong saw smoke curling up and he heard a confused shouting.

In the street where Tala lived a motley crowd barred his way. A few dozen Tartars were jostling one another, shouting and cursing. Three Indians were throwing lighted torches on the roof of the house, acclaimed by the slatternly women standing in the doorways of the houses opposite. Ma Joong let his heavy whip descend on the bare, sweat-covered backs of the nearest Tartars, then forced his horse right among them. Shouting angrily, the crowd turned round towards him. When they recognized the uniform of an officer of the tribunal, they fell back in sullen silence.

Ma Joong jumped from his horse and ran over to the woman lying at the base of the mud wall beside the door. Tala's long cloak was torn into ribbons, soaked with blood, and there were ugly gashes on the white arms with which she was protecting her face. Broken sticks and stones were lying all around her. As Ma Joong knelt by her side, a brick swished past his head and hit the wall with a thud. He turned round and saw a half-naked Tartar stooping to pick up another brick. Quick as lightning, Ma Joong sprang up and was on him. He grabbed the man's long scalp with his left and let the butt end of his whip descend on the nape of his neck. Throwing the limp body down, he shouted at the crowd:

'Get water buckets and put out the fire. Do you want all your houses to burn down?'

160

Tala had let her arms drop away from her face. A gaping wound ran across her brow, and the left side of her face was crushed to a pulp.

'I'll put you on my horse and take you to . . .' Ma Joong began.

She fixed him with her one, bloodshot eye.

'Burn . . . my body,' she whispered.

Suddenly there was a crash, followed by screams of terror from the crowd. The roof of Tala's house had caved in. The large head of the fierce deity became visible. The statue's red face seemed even more horribly distorted by the flames that blazed up all around it.

Ma Joong gathered the woman in his arms and stepped away from the wall, for pieces of burning wood were coming down from the roof. He saw her bleeding lips move.

'Scatter my ashes . . .' she said, nearly inaudibly. He felt her shiver, then her body grew limp in his arms.

He laid the dead woman on his horse. The Tartar he had felled had been carried away by his friends. The others were kneeling, facing Tala's house, in abject fear. The burning head of the statue looked down on them with a sardonic smile.

'Get up and put the fire out, you fools!' Ma Joong shouted at them.

Then he swung onto his horse and rode back to the tribunal with the dead woman.

Judge Dee received the news calmly. Giving Ma Joong and the sergeant a grave look, he said, 'Tala was a fey woman from the time she embraced the creed that leads to perdition. My orders are not to interfere with the religious squabbles of the foreign barbarians, so we shall take no action against the people living in that quarter. We shall have her body cremated at once, as she desired.'

161

He was interrupted by the booming sound of the large gong at the gate of the tribunal. Coming at that moment, it reminded the judge of the gong in a Buddhist temple, sounded at the end of the service for the dead, to usher the soul of the deceased to the other world.

'The session is about to begin,' he said. 'You had better go and have a rest, Ma Joong; for in the afternoon we shall search the temple. You'll assist me in court, Sergeant. I am afraid it'll again be a long session, for the case Kao vs Lo is coming up for re-examination; now the Lo side want to bring up their new evidence. At the end of the session I shall order the release of the vagabond Ah-liu. Get my official robe out, Hoong.'

After Ma Joong had issued the necessary orders for the burning of Tala's corpse, he went straight to the guard-house. He stripped naked, squatted on a corner of the stone floor, and had two guards pour buckets of cold water over him. Then he went up to his small attic, naked as he was, and threw himself down on his military plank bed. He was very tired, for, having gone to the Hermitage before dawn, he had had but a few hours' sleep after the strenuous night in the temple. However, as soon as he had closed his eyes, the horribly mutilated face of Tala rose before his mind's eye; then he saw her again as she had stood before him, naked over the heap of skulls. . . . Muttering curses he tossed about till at last he fell into a dreamless sleep.

He woke up with a splitting headache. A glance out of the window proved that it was already late in the afternoon. He quickly dressed and went downstairs. While he was gulping down a bowl of cold noodles in the guardroom a constable told him that the senior scribe had come back from Tong-kang. He had just passed the gate, on his way to Judge Dee's office.

Ma Joong set the bowl down and hurried to the chancery.

Judge Dee was sitting behind his desk, the sergeant was standing by his side. The old scribe sat on the chair opposite, as always looking very neat and prim. Sitting down, Ma Joong cast an astonished look at the many small slips of notepaper arranged in neat rows on the desk, each covered with Judge Dee's familiar bold handwriting. On top of the array lay seven large cards, generally used for marking a spot in a dossier. He tried to apologize for his lateness, but Judge Dee raised his hand. 'You are just in time to hear the report on Tong-kang, Ma Joong.' And, to the old scribe, he said, 'Continue!'

'The commander of the military convoy kindly let me join them, sir, and so I travelled the greater part of the way back in comfort, and fast too! The last stretch I did on horseback, with a group of tea merchants. We rode on all night. We were lucky, for when the rain storm broke we found shelter in the hut of a woodgatherer on the second mountain ridge. Then—'

'You had quite a journey,' the judge interrupted. 'Just give me the gist of what you learned in Tong-kang. You can draw up a detailed report later, after you have taken a rest.'

'Thank you, sir. I want to begin by stating that the chancery personnel of the tribunal in Tong-kang treated me most courteously. They assigned to me most comfortable quarters in the hostel for official travellers.'

'I shall write my colleague a letter of thanks. What did you learn about the Treasurer's stay there?'

'My colleagues introduced me to the clerk who had been ordered to look after the Treasurer's needs, sir. He told me his had been an easy task, for the Treasurer had

163

been tired by the long journey, and declined the magistrate's invitation to dinner. When the clerk was serving the evening rice in the Treasurer's room, the latter told him to have a leather worker called, for one of his travelling boxes was developing a crack. After the leather worker had gone, the Treasurer retired. He received no other visitors, and left the next morning at dawn.'

The old scribe made a bow to the sergeant, who had pushed a cup of tea towards him. After he had taken a few sips, he resumed, 'The headman of the tribunal found that leather worker for me. His name is Liu, an elderly, rather garrulous person. He began his career as a goldsmith, but then his eyes went bad and he shifted to the tooling of leather. He remembered his visit to the Treasurer quite well, because a few days later he heard that the gold had been stolen and—'

'Yes, yes, naturally. What happened during that visit?'

'Well, sir, the Treasurer took Liu to his bedroom and showed him the box that was cracking. Liu examined it, and told the Treasurer that the leather was of such good quality that he needn't fear that it would burst. The Treasurer was visibly relieved and gave Liu a good tip. Encouraged by the kind words of this high official, Liu praised the workmanship of a gold ornament the Treasurer was wearing, adding that he was really a goldsmith. The Treasurer said that in that case he had more work for him. He took an intricate key from his sleeve, and opened the padlock of the cracked box. He had stood himself with his back to Liu, but Liu saw in the cap-mirror on the table that the box was filled to the rim with heavy gold bars. The Treasurer closed the box and turned round to Liu with one large bar in his hand. He told Liu that it was unusually long; he had forced it into the box on top of his clothes, he said, and that was probably the reason why the box had got cracked. He asked Liu whether he could saw it for him into two pieces, without losing any of the gold-dust. Liu had the right kind of saw in his tool box, and he left directly after having done the job. That's all, sir!'

Judge Dee gave his two lieutenants a significant look. He asked the scribe, 'Whom did Liu tell about his discovery?'

'Oh, dozens of people, Your Honour! It so happened that the Guild of the Gold- and Silversmiths had its regular meeting that very night, and Liu told the gathering his story. It isn't often the common people hear about such a large gold transport, and they had a good time developing all kinds of theories about the reason why an Imperial Treasurer would be taking such a large sum over the border.'

'You did excellent work! After you have refreshed yourself, you had better have a look at the records of the court sessions of yesterday and today. The case Kao vs Lo came up again, you know.'

'I certainly want to see those records, sir!' the old gentleman said eagerly. 'Yes, I had suspected that both sides kept a few tricks up their sleeve, especially the Kao side! There's that obscure point about the second marriage of the third cousin, and—'

'Here are the two dossiers,' Judge Dee told him hastily. 'I shall hear the case again tomorrow.'

The old scribe left, fondly clasping the two dossiers in his arms.

'The Treasurer made a fatal mistake,' the sergeant remarked. 'He should have told Liu to leave the room for a few moments, while he took the gold bar from the box.'

'Of course,' Ma Joong put in. 'It doesn't get us much

further, though. How can we find out which one of those guildsmen took the news to Lan-fang? It may have been a friend, or—'

'That's immaterial, Ma Joong,' Judge Dee interrupted. 'The main point is that now we know for certain how the secret leaked out, that the news was brought here before the Treasurer arrived, and that it became known in the milieu of goldsmiths and metal-workers. That's all I need.'

'Are we going to the deserted temple now, sir?' Ma Joong asked. 'There are six guards up there, but I don't like the idea of all that gold lying around!'

'No, we aren't going there just yet. As I was explaining to the sergeant before our scribe came in, Ma Joong, I have now completed a theory about our case. It necessitated a careful re-examination of all the evidence which has come to light so far, and especially a painstaking check on dates. Dates play a vital part in all this, Ma Joong. Hence all those slips of paper you see here before me. The results I summed up on those seven cards which I put on top. On each card I wrote down a name, together with some significant facts. These slips don't matter any more.'

The judge pulled the drawer out and swept the slips inside with the tip of his sleeve.

'We shall now examine together these seven cards. I turned them face down when the arrival of our scribe was announced, for the old gentleman has good eyes! And each card bears the name of a suspected murderer.'

XIX

Judge Dee straightened up in his chair. Folding his arms, he resumed, 'Before explaining why I suspect these seven people, severally or in pairs, I must first tell you that we have only one single case. The day before yesterday—Heavens, that seems ages ago now!—we thought we had three entirely different cases. Two dating from nearly one year back: namely, the theft of the Treasurer's gold, and the mysterious message of a woman called Jade; and a third dating from the night before, namely, Seng-san's murder in the deserted temple. Subsequent developments showed that the theft of the gold was connected with the murders in the temple, and this morning the floor-plan, drawn by the maid of the Abbess, convinced me that Miss Jade's disappearance must be linked up with the crimes committed there. We have only one single case, my friends, but a case with many ramifications! It all began with the theft of the Treasurer's gold. Around those fifty stolen gold bars developed a curious, most intricate web of conflicting human passions. Pour me another cup, Hoong!'

The judge emptied the cup in a few quick gulps. Then he rummaged in his drawer and took out a sheet of paper.

'A few moments ago I remarked that dates provide

important clues in this case. I have jotted down a few here. Have a look!'

The sergeant and Ma Joong drew their chairs closer to the desk and read what Judge Dee had written.

Fifteen years ago (the year of the Hare):

> The authorities close down the Temple of the Purple Clouds; the Hermitage is built, and placed in charge of a priest and priestess who had forsworn the new creed.

Last year (the year of the Snake):

> 15-V Marriage of Mr and Mrs Woo.
> 2-VIII The Treasurer's gold is stolen.
> 20-VIII The widow Chang becomes Abbess of the Hermitage.
> 6-IX Ming Ao disappears.
> 10-IX Miss Jade disappears.
> 12-IX Date of Miss Jade's message.

Ma Joong looked up. 'Who's Ming Ao, sir?'

'Don't you remember what Sergeant Hoong told you about his examination of the file of missing persons, the day before yesterday? He had found there that the brother of a metal-worker called Ming Ao reported that Ming had gone out on the night of the sixth day of the ninth month and never came back. Now, Lee Mai told us that Mrs Woo had lived with a metal-worker who left her about one year ago. This afternoon I had the sergeant make discreet inquiries from Ming Ao's brother, and Hoong elicited from him that the present Mrs Woo had indeed lived with Ming Ao for some time. Ming Ao was known as an expert locksmith and a skilful metal-worker. But he was a crook—exactly as Lee Mai

168

said when he told us about Mrs Woo's former acquaint-ances. Anyway, keep these dates and names in mind! They are of vital importance.'

He leaned forward and turned up the first card.

'This card I marked Woo Tsung-jen, the retired prefect. Woo remained an honest man all through his long official career. But in his later years, after he had become poor and married a wicked woman, his character changed. Here, this second card bears Mrs Woo's name. I lay it beside that of her husband. You'll agree that this pair were in an excellent position for hearing the news about the gold from Tong-kang. Woo frequented Lee Mai's shop, and Mrs Woo's lover was a metal-worker. When they hear the news from Tong-kang, they realize that here is the chance of a life-time. Mrs Woo contacts her former lover Ming Ao, and he steals the gold and re-places it by lead; this last touch was probably suggested by Woo. Ming Ao conceals the gold somewhere in the de-serted temple. Then, however, a complication arises. Ming Ao refuses to reveal where exactly he has hidden the gold. Was he angry because his mistress had married? Or was it just because he wanted all the gold for himself? We can only guess at the answers to those questions. One thing is certain, however: Mr and Mrs Woo don't take Ming Ao's refusal lying down. They press him, torture him perhaps. Four days later he is killed, and his dead body is spirited away. Now the pair begin a systematic search of the temple. For many months they search, without result. Then a second complication occurs. Yang worms the secret of the gold out of Mrs Woo—there are strong indications that they were lovers—or he learns it while spying on Woo. Yang hires Seng-san to blackmail the Woos. They lure Yang and Seng-san to the temple, and there they murder them.'

'If that theory is correct,' Ma Joong exclaimed, 'then Mrs Woo is that blasted phantom! But what about Miss Jade?'

'I think that Jade discovered that her father and step-mother had murdered Ming Ao, and they decided that Jade had to go too, and at once. Her stepmother hated her, and her demise delivered her father from a guilty passion that had long tormented him. Well, the activities Mr and Mrs Woo engaged in yesterday fully support this theory. My proclamation badly frightened the guilty couple. Had I found a clue to their having murdered the girl? Am I about to summon them for questioning? They decide that attack is the best defence. Woo rushes to me, Mrs Woo to my Third Lady, in a desperate effort to learn what I have discovered, and to confuse the issue.

'However, there is one flaw in my argument, and a very important one too. Woo could well have thrown the stones on you in the well, Ma Joong, and he could also have pushed the upper part of the crumbling back wall of the temple over. But I don't see how he, an elderly gentleman, could ever have strangled Yang and knifed Seng-san; how he could have moved Seng-san's body, and how he could have eluded you in the dark temple hall. Have you any comment, Sergeant?'

When Hoong shook his head, the judge continued, 'I turn up my third card. Lee Mai, the banker. The most likely person to hear the news from Tong-kang, of course. We know that Mrs Woo didn't live exactly like a nun before her marriage to Woo. She may well have carried on with Lee Mai, with or without Ming Ao's knowledge. When Woo falls in love with her, Lee Mai encourages the match: nothing more convenient than marry off your mistress to your best friend! Woo wants to give his

JUDGE DEE DISCUSSES SEVEN CARDS

daughter Jade in marriage to Lee. So much the better! Lee will have a nice young wife, and at the same time have even better opportunities for continuing the liaison with her stepmother. Lee Mai and Mrs Woo organize the theft of the gold by Ming Ao. Then the two snags I mentioned before occur again: Ming refuses to reveal the hiding-place of the gold, and they murder him. Jade discovers that murder, or her stepmother's adultery, and she is eliminated. Mrs Woo hates her, and Lee prefers a fortune in gold to a young wife. As to the double murder in the temple, Lee Mai is a tall strong man, fond of hunting. A worthy opponent for you in the dark hall, Ma Joong! Any objections, Sergeant?'

Sergeant Hoong had been looking rather dubious. Now he said, 'How do we reconcile this theory with Lee Mai's attempt at blackening Mrs Woo, sir? He went out of his way to point out to us her questionable background.'

'That may have been a clever touch, meant to throw us off the scent. Lee knew very well that we hadn't got a shred of evidence against her. And he had told her exactly what she was to tell my Third Lady. Well, we have had now two men and one woman. This fourth card is a woman again. I turn it over and lay it beside that of Lee Mai.'

Sergeant Hoong leaned forward. He gasped as he read the name. 'The Abbess!' he exclaimed.

'Yes, the Abbess. Remember that she was the widow of a gold merchant, and would know Lee Mai, her husband's colleague. What if she and Lee Mai had become secret lovers? The records say that her husband died in the first month of the year of the Snake, of a sudden heart attack. Did he discover her adultery with Lee, and did the couple help him to leave this mortal world? The circumstances of Mr Chang's demise will

172

bear looking into, I think. Anyway, it is significant that, in the very same month that the gold was stolen, she became Abbess of the Hermitage—an ideal position for a person interested in the deserted temple who wants to search for concealed gold undisturbed! Finally, she knew beforehand that you, Ma Joong, were going to visit the temple. I told her so myself, during the birthday dinner. And she left very early, as soon as the last course had been served. Because she had a headache, she said.'

'So she could easily have been back in the temple in time to lure me to the well,' Ma Joong remarked bitterly. 'And last night, after she had helped to set the trap for me under the crumbling wall, she had plenty of time to get back to the Hermitage while I was trying to catch Lee in the temple hall. But what about Jade, sir?'

'Same story as before: Jade must have caught them red-handed when they were disposing of Ming Ao.'

'The Abbess might even have enjoyed killing the poor girl.' Ma Joong said nastily. 'Her maid told me that the cruel bitch positively enjoys caning her! But what exactly could have happened to Jade, sir?'

'According to Tala,' the judge replied slowly, 'Miss Jade broke her neck. And on the tenth, on the same day that she disappeared. According to the message in the ebony box, however, she died on or about the twelfth.'

'The date of her message of distress fits,' Sergeant Hoong remarked. 'She was kept captive from the tenth till the twelfth, without food or drink!'

Judge Dee took up the fifth card.

'This one I inscribed with the name of Lee Ko, the painter. Look, I put his card in between those of Mrs Woo and the Abbess. Now then. Lee Ko had as good an opportunity to learn the secret of the gold as his brother Lee Mai, because then he was still living in the banker's

173

house. For the same reason he could have met Ming Ao and the woman who became Mrs Woo.'

The judge moved Lee Ko's card close to that of Mrs Woo, and regarded the two with a satisfied smile. 'I must confess that I like this combination! I like it very much indeed. The sensual woman married to an elderly husband, and the irresponsible painter who believes in romantic love. And both nearing middle-age, when passion burns with a more intense fire than in one's youth.'

'Lee Ko also knew that I was going to visit the temple,' Ma Joong muttered. 'I told him so when I met him on my way to the east city gate. And Lee had the ebony box in his possession! Besides, he is a mountaineer, a hardy chap! That's why he gave such a good account of himself when I tried to catch him in the temple hall!'

Judge Dee nodded. He moved Lee Ko's card closer to that of the Abbess. 'This combination,' he said, 'is decidedly less attractive. But we must remember that Lee Ko painted those awful Buddhist pictures most expertly. He must have made a close study of the originals that were formerly displayed in the deserted temple; and there he may have met the Abbess, who was already a fervent Buddhist when she was still Mrs Chang. Well, I take the sixth card. You see that I have put Yang's name there.'

'Yang is dead!' the sergeant exclaimed.

'We shouldn't ignore the dead, Hoong—to borrow one of Tala's pronouncements. I put Yang's card on top of Lee Ko's, and then I put Mrs Woo's card beside it. Look, now we have a combination that is even more plausible than that of Mrs Woo and Lee Ko! A frustrated, sensual woman and a much younger, gay student, living under the same roof! She'll have told Yang about the gold, and

174

made him do the rough work. We saw Yang's dead body; he was a strong fellow who could have easily handled both Ming Ao and Miss Jade.'

'But later Yang himself was murdered, together with Seng-san!' Sergeant Hoong protested.

'Precisely! That's why I laid Yang's card on top of that of Lee Ko. For in the course of the months that followed the theft, the pattern changed. Mrs Woo fell in love with Lee Ko. She told Yang that she was through with him, and that he could say goodbye to the gold. But Yang wouldn't stand for that. He went to Lee Ko and told him that he didn't care a tinker's curse about Mrs Woo, but that he wanted his half of the gold. In order to keep an eye on the pair, Yang forced Lee Ko to employ him, threatening to tell everything to old Mr Woo. Then, however, Yang realized that Lee Ko was not a man to be trifled with, and he decided to try to get the gold by himself, all of it. So he hired Seng-san, the professional bully, who'd help him to search the deserted temple. There they were murdered by Lee Ko and Mrs Woo.'

Judge Dee picked up the six cards. Leaning back in his chair, he shuffled them and said, 'There are, of course, a few other possible combinations. But we have now surveyed, I think, the essential patterns we must reckon with.'

'There's still one more card on the table, sir,' the sergeant said.

The judge sat up straight. 'Ah yes, the seventh card!' He turned it over. It was black.

Holding it up, he said slowly:

'I had written a name there, tentatively. Perhaps the name of a phantom. The Phantom of the Temple. Then, however, I blacked it out. This card means death.'

He stuck the black card among the others, reshuffled them, and threw the package in his open drawer. He folded his arms and resumed, 'Ordinarily we should, now that we have arrived at this stage, initiate a laborious and time-consuming investigation. We should trace in detail the antecedents of all our suspects, find out where and with whom they were at the time the various crimes were committed, question domestic servants, shopkeepers, etc. That would take weeks, if not months, even if our friends Chiao Tai and Tao Gan were here to take part in the investigation. Fortunately, we are in a position to take a short-cut.' He pulled the floor-plan drawn by Spring Cloud towards him. Tapping it with his forefinger, he resumed, 'Thanks to this excellent sketch, we can conduct this very night a decisive test.

'Half an hour ago, I had a clerk deliver two letters. One addressed to Mr and Mrs Woo, the other to their friend Lee Mai, the banker. I invited them to come to the deserted temple in two hours' time, because I wanted to tell them there the results of my inquiries regarding Miss Jade.'

'What about Lee Ko and the Abbess, sir?' Ma Joong asked.

'The Abbess I shall fetch personally from the Hermitage. I want to go there anyway, to see how young Fang is getting along. As regards Lee Ko, you'll go to his house now, Ma Joong. Tell him that I ordered you to take him to the deserted temple, because I want to show him there something without anyone else knowing about it, to ask his opinion. Take him up the hill by the back road, for he should on no account see that I have other guests too. Keep him waiting behind the temple. When I need him, I shall let you know. Then you'll bring him into the hall by the small back door.' As Ma Joong rose, the judge added quickly, 'Watch him all the time, Ma Joong! He is a murder suspect!'

'I'll watch him all right!' the tall man said grimly as he went out. Judge Dee got up too. 'Come along, Hoong! I must be there before my guests arrive. I want to test my theory before I test my suspects!'

XX

The guards at the east gate stared, astonished, at the official cortège. First came two constables on horseback who beat small brass gongs and shouted, 'Make way, make way! His Excellency the Magistrate is approaching!' Then came two others, each carrying on a pole a large lampion of oil-paper, marked in red letters 'The Tribunal of Lan-fang'. After them followed Judge Dee's official palankeen, carried by ten uniformed bearers. The headman rode beside the palankeen, and twelve mounted guards brought up the rear.

When the coolies, loafers and beggars sitting at the street stalls that lined the road outside the gate saw the cortège, they got up to join it. The headman shouted at them to stay behind, but the palankeen's window-curtain was raised. Judge Dee looked out and told the headman:

'Let them come if they want to!'

Judge Dee and Sergeant Hoong descended from the palankeen at the bottom of the staircase. Remembering the stiff climb ahead, the judge had not put on his official costume, but chosen a robe of thin grey cotton with black borders and a broad black sash. On his head he wore a high square cap of black gauze.

In the front courtyard of the temple the constables stuck the poles with the lampions of the tribunal in the ground, on either side of the triple entrance gate. The judge told them to wait there. He went on to the main hall, accompanied only by Sergeant Hoong, the headman and the senior constable; the latter carried two lanterns, a rope ladder, and a coil of thin cord.

They remained a long time in the hall. When Judge Dee came down into the front yard again, his face was pale and drawn in the light of the lampions. He told the headman curtly to receive his guests, and order them to wait in the front courtyard. The constables were to place torches in the temple hall and to sweep the floor. Having issued these orders, he went with Sergeant Hoong along the path that led to the Hermitage.

When the Abbess herself opened the gate, the judge thanked her warmly for taking care of the wounded constable, and said he wished to see him. The Abbess took them to a small side hall of the chapel, where Fang was lying on a bamboo bed. Spring Cloud was squatting in the corner by a brazier, fanning the glowing coals under a medicine jar. Judge Dee praised the young constable for having spotted the buried head and wished him a speedy recovery.

'I am being looked after very well indeed, Your Honour,' Fang said gratefully. 'The Abbess has dressed the wound, and every two hours Spring Cloud gives me a dose of medicine that keeps the fever down.' Sergeant Hoong noticed the fond glance the young constable bestowed on Spring Cloud, and he saw her blush.

Back in the front yard Judge Dee said to the Abbess, 'Tonight I have invited a few people to the deserted temple for a general discussion of the murder that took place there recently. I would like you to be present too. This area belongs to your religious jurisdiction, so to speak!'

The Abbess made no comment. She inclined her head in assent, pulled the hood closer to her head, and followed the judge and Sergeant Hoong outside.

Mr Woo was pacing the yard, his hands clasped behind his back. He had put on for this occasion a dark-green robe with broad black borders and a high black cap that gave him a very official appearance. His wife, dressed in a dark robe and with a black veil draped over her hair, was sitting on a large boulder. Mr Lee Mai was standing by her side.

Judge Dee ceremoniously introduced Mr Woo and Mr Lee to the Abbess. It turned out that the Abbess knew Mrs Woo already, the latter having visited the Hermitage a few times to burn incense. Standing in the centre of the front yard, they exchanged the usual polite inquiries. The mellow light of the two large lanterns made the grey walls of the temple appear less forbidding. If it had not been for the constables and guards standing about near the gate, this could have been a social gathering, organized in the temple yard to enjoy the evening cool.

'I am most grateful to all of you for having come here at such short notice,' the judge addressed them. 'Now I want you to come with me to the main hall. There I shall explain why I wanted you to be present here tonight.'

He crossed the yard. The six-fold doors were thrown open and they entered the main hall, now brilliantly lit by numerous large torches. The constables had stuck those into the old holes in the wall, bored there for that purpose. Walking up to the altar table in the rear, Judge Dee thought that, in the old days, when the walls were still covered with gorgeous religious pictures, and the altar loaded with all the ritual paraphernalia, this hall must have presented a most impressive appearance. He went to stand with his back against the altar table, and motioned Mr and Mrs Woo to the place directly in front of him. Then he asked the Abbess to stand on their right, Mr Lee Mai on their left. In the meantime the headman had gone to the left end of the altar table, the senior constable to the right. They stood stiffly at attention there. Sergeant Hoong stayed in the background by the pillars, together with six guards.

The judge surveyed the four people in front of him with sombre eyes, slowly stroking his long black beard. Then he addressed Mr Woo, saying gravely:

'I deeply regret that I have to inform you that your daughter Jade is dead. She died here in this hall.'

Having thus spoken, he quickly walked away to the left. Passing the headman he barked at him, 'Move the table!'

The headman gripped the left end of the altar table with both hands, and the constable at the other side did the same. Judge Dee looked sharply at the four people in front of the table. Mr and Mrs Woo exchanged a bewildered glance. Lee Mai stared at the judge with raised eyebrows. The Abbess stood rigidly erect, watching the headman and the constable with her large, vacant eyes. They had tilted the table a little, then frozen in that attitude.

After a brief, uncomfortable pause, Judge Dee told the headman, 'That'll do!'

As they let the table fall back, the judge resumed his former position in front of it. Again he addressed Mr Woo.

'Your daughter, Mr Woo, had become infatuated with your secretary, Mr Yang Mou-te. You can't blame her for that. She lost her mother at the age she needed her most, and too much reading had given her romantic notions. She was an easy victim for an experienced, dissolute young man like Yang. Give her memory a place in your heart, Mr Woo. After she had told you that fateful night, she ran out of the house. Not to her aunt, but all the way to this deserted temple. For she knew that Yang often came here. She wanted to tell him that you had refused to let her marry him and wanted to take counsel with him about what they should do. However, Yang was not here that night. She found here another man. A murderer, who was just looking at the result of his heinous crime.

'This man had organized the theft of the Imperial Treasurer's fifty gold bars, stolen here nearly one year ago, on the second day of the eighth month of the year of the Snake. For breaking into the Treasurer's room and stealing the gold, he had employed a skilled metal-worker and locksmith, a man called Ming Ao.'

There was a stifled cry. Mrs Woo quickly clasped her hand to her mouth. Her husband shot her an astonished look and went to ask her something. But Judge Dee raised his hand.

'You are aware of the fact, Mr Woo, that, before you married her, your wife had a difficult life. At one time she knew Ming Ao. His brother reported to the tribunal that he had disappeared on the sixth day of the ninth month. That was five weeks after the theft of the gold, and four days before the disappearance of your daughter, Mr Woo. Ming Ao's principal had ordered him to conceal the gold here in the deserted temple, and Ming had hidden it expertly, for he was a skilful locksmith, familiar with secret wall-safes, camouflaged hiding-places and all such devices. He thought he was entitled to more than the share promised and refused to tell his principal exactly where he had hidden the gold. I assume that at first his principal tried to make Ming Ao tell by promises, and,

182

PREFECT WOO AND THE ABBESS BEFORE JUDGE DEE

when those didn't work, by threats, and, when—'

'All this seems immaterial to me,' Mr Woo interrupted impatiently. 'I want to know who murdered my daughter, and how.'

Judge Dee turned to the banker, Lee Mai.

'The murderer was your brother, the painter Lee Ko.'

Lee Mai's round face went pale.

'My . . . my brother?' he stammered. 'I knew that he was no good. . . . But Heavens, a murder . . .'

'Your brother,' the judge continued, 'must have frequented this temple for years, to study the Buddhist pictures here. Somehow or other he must have learned of the existence of a deep crypt under this altar. As you know, most larger temples have such a secret crypt, to store their valuable ritual objects during times of upheaval, and as hide-out for the inmates. Lee Ko must have tricked Ming Ao into descending into that crypt, then told him he would let him starve there if he didn't reveal the hiding-place of the gold. This happened on the night of the sixth of the ninth month, the night Ming Ao disappeared. Four days later. on the tenth, Lee Ko opened the crypt. He had left Ming Ao there too long; the locksmith had died—without having revealed the secret. Your daughter, Mr Woo, found Lee Ko standing by the open crypt, and he threw her inside. Their bodies are still there. Please stand back, all of you! Yes, that'll do.' Judge Dee went over to the side where the headman stood, and told him curtly: 'Open the crypt!'

Again the headman and his assistant tilted the altar table. Then, with an obvious effort, they pushed it away from the wall, inch by inch. When the distance was five inches, a section of the stone floor measuring six feet square suddenly rose, rotating round an axis located along the foot of the wall, where the altar table had stood. A nauseating smell of decay rose up from the gaping dark hole.

On a sign from the judge, the headman lit a lantern that had a long thin rope attached to it. While he let it down into the crypt, the judge motioned Mr Woo to come to the rim. Together they looked down.

The perfectly smooth brick wall went down for nearly twenty feet. Deep down below lay a mass of rubbish: smaller and larger wooden boxes, a few earthenware jars, and broken candlesticks. At the left were the remains of a woman, lying on her back. The long hair lay around the skull like an aureole, bones were sticking up from the remnants of a decaying brown robe. On the other side, close to the wall, were the remains of a man, lying face down, his arms flung outward. Through the holes in the torn, mould-covered sleeves pieces of gold were sparkling in the lantern's light.

'I went down there with a rope-ladder,' Judge Dee spoke. His voice came muffled through the neckcloth he had pulled up over his nose and mouth. 'In the wall directly above Ming Ao's body there is a cleverly made secret wall-safe. In the last, terrible moments Ming Ao spent here he opened this safe and, half-crazed by hunger and thirst, began to take out the gold bars he had hidden there and stuff them into his sleeves. Then he fell down, dead. On top of the rest of the gold, which had dropped onto the floor. Before the murderer had put Ming Ao in the crypt, he had, of course, examined it carefully, as the most obvious place for hiding the gold. But he had failed to locate the secret wall-safe. And when he opened the crypt and found Ming Ao dead, he didn't see the gold. That we can see it now from up here is because Ming Ao's gown has decayed and been eaten by worms. So, the murderer didn't know that the gold was here, and he began a long and fruitless search of the temple.'

Mr Woo stepped back, his face ashen.

'Where is the cruel fiend who did my poor daughter to death?' he asked hoarsely.

Judge Dee nodded at the headman. He left the hall by the narrow back door. Then the judge pointed at the trap door.

'As you see, this trap door is made of extremely thick wooden logs. They are covered with a layer of cement, and the stone slabs are added on top of that. The door is so heavy that, when closed, there is no hollow sound even when one stamps one's foot on it. At the other end there's a counterweight, underground outside. Two wedges hold it on balance. If the altar table is tilted, then pushed forward in a line perfectly parallel to the wall, the wedges are released. A very clever piece of workmanship.'

The headman came inside with a tall man. Ma Joong followed close behind.

As soon as the man saw the open crypt and the people standing there, he covered his face with his arm. Too late.

'Yang!' Mrs Woo cried out. 'What—'

The man swung round, but Ma Joong grabbed him and pinned his arms down in a wrestler's lock. The headman put him in chains.

Yang's tall body sagged. He remained standing there with downcast eyes, his face a deadly pale.

'Where's my brother?' Lee Mai shouted.

'Your brother is dead, Mr Lee,' the judge said softly. 'He committed two murders, and was murdered himself in turn.' He gave the headman a peremptory sign. Together with the senior constable, he moved the table back to its original place against the wall. Slowly the trap door closed again. Judge Dee resumed his place in front of the altar table.

186

'You are entitled to hear the full story, Mr Lee. I take up the thread of my narrative. Since your brother is dead, part of what I am going to say is conjecture. But Yang Mou-te will fill in the gaps. Well, after Lee Ko had killed Ming Ao and Miss Jade, he began to search the temple. Since he knew that all kinds of riff-raff frequented it at night and since his search would have to include also the garden, he needed help. So he took Yang in his service. How much did Lee Ko tell you, Yang?'

The chained man looked up with dazed eyes.

'He said that the monks had hidden a treasure there,' he mumbled. 'I . . . I suspected there was more to it. I found in Lee's bedroom notes of calculation on the value of fifty gold bars, and . . .'

'And you thought you could do better for yourself than the share Lee had promised you,' Judge Dee broke in upon his words. 'You hired the professional bully Seng-san, and together you worked out a plan for luring Lee to the temple and murdering him. Seng-san strangled Lee from behind. Then you executed the second phase of your fiendish plan, Yang. You waited till Seng-san had choked the life out of Lee, and stood bent over his victim. Then you plunged your knife into Seng-san's back. Why did you wait weeks on end before murdering Lee? Then why did you try twice to murder my lieutenant on two successive nights? Why didn't you wait a few days, till we had given up the search of the temple? Speak up, Yang!'

Yang's lips moved, but no sound came forth.

'Tell the truth!' the judge barked.

'Last week . . . I went through Lee's papers again when he was out. He used to go to the old bookshops, nearly every day. . . . At last he found what he was looking for. A collection of letters, written by an

187

abbot of the temple, more than a hundred years ago. One letter dealt with the building of a secret wall-safe, down in the crypt. When Lee bought a rope-ladder . . . I had to be very quick, for I couldn't impersonate Lee longer than a few days at most. I had to get the gold quickly, leave here . . .'

'Tomorrow you shall render a full account of your crimes in court,' Judge Dee interrupted. 'Take the prisoner away, headman, and let six guards convey him to jail! Mr Woo, yesterday you asked me what new clues to your daughter's disappearance prompted me to issue a proclamation. I shall now answer your question. There came into my hands a note signed with your daughter's name, stating that she was being kept captive here, and begging someone to rescue her. It was enclosed in an antique ebony box. The cover of that box was decorated with a disc of green jade, carved into the shape of a stylized, archaic form of the character for "long life". Someone had scratched at one side of that character the word "entrance" and at the other side the word "below". Now it so happens that the shape of that character bears a close resemblance to the floor-plan of this very temple. The oblong space in the centre suggests the main hall, the dented lines beside it the cells of the monks, the two squares the two towers. The box was evidently chosen because of this resemblance; it supplemented the information of the message. The message stated the time, the box the place. And the place was indicated exactly by the word "below" scratched beside the back wall of the hall: it clearly pointed to a crypt, under the altar.'

'My daughter must have found the box in the crypt,' Woo muttered. 'But how did she . . .'

Judge Dee shook his head.

'The message inside was signed with your daughter's

name, Mr Woo, but she didn't write it. The fall into this deep crypt broke her neck, and she died at once. The box was an elaborate hoax, contrived for reasons not germane to the present issue. The hoax helped me, however, to reconstruct the crime, for it drew my attention to the crypt here. The box was allegedly found near a rabbit hole, on the slope behind the temple. That points to the mouth of an airshaft. This crypt has indeed four air-shafts, to prevent the monks from suffocating when they had to take refuge there for a few days. The large jars in the crypt contained water and dried rice. I shan't detain you any longer, Mr Woo. I shall have the remains of your daughter properly encoffined, and delivered to you for burial. I deeply regret that her life could not be saved. But Heaven has punished her murderer. And the doubts her disappearance caused you have now been resolved.'

Mr Woo made a low bow. Then he turned and strode to the entrance, followed by his wife. The judge quickly overtook her. He told her in a low voice:

'Yesterday your husband didn't come to the tribunal to denounce you, Mrs Woo. He wanted to protect you. Now you can start your married life anew. Don't look for cheap amusement on the side. You have seen that it may lead to ignominious death.'

She nodded and quickly walked on to join her husband.

When Judge Dee had gone back to the altar, he saw that Lee Mai was standing there, his head down, staring at the closed trap door.

'Please accept the expression of my sincerest sympathy, Mr Lee.'

The banker bowed.

'I mourn my fiancée, sir. I had always hoped that she

189   G*

was still alive. And I am deeply distressed by my brother's bringing dishonour over our family.'

'I have a great respect for your firm character and your unswerving loyalty, Mr Lee,' the judge said gravely. 'A family that counts among its members a man like you should weather all reverses.'

Lee Mai bowed again and crossed the hall to the entrance.

The Abbess, who had been watching all this with her large, vacant eyes, now slowly shook her head and said, 'This temple was destined to become the scene of terrible events, for it has been desecrated by heterodox rites. And where the Lord Buddha leaves, evil spirits and devils come to dwell. I shall at once make preparations for an elaborate purification ceremony. Goodbye, sir.'

'See Her Reverence home, Ma Joong!' Judge Dee ordered. Then he turned to the headman. 'Send four of your men to the east city gate, to fetch bamboo ladders, two temporary coffins, spades, shovels and more ropes. We shall first remove the dead bodies, then the gold. Finally the crypt must be cleaned out. Let's go outside and wait in the yard, Hoong. The musty atmosphere here has become unbearable!'

The judge sat down on a large boulder under one of the lampions of the tribunal, Sergeant Hoong on a tree trunk. From the other side of the outer wall came a confused murmur of voices. The beggars and loafers who had followed the cortège from the east gate had eagerly questioned the guards who took the prisoner away. Now they were busily discussing the astonishing developments.

Sergeant Hoong gratefully inhaled the fresh air. He tried to sort out the events that had followed one another in such quick succession, but he couldn't put all the pieces together; it seemed to him that Judge Dee had deliberately left some lacunae. The main point was, however, that the judge had recovered the Treasurer's gold! He smiled contentedly. This would certainly make the high authorities in the capital favourably disposed to the judge. It might mean promotion to a better post than this out-of-the-way, provincial district!

'How are you going to transport the government gold, sir?' he asked.

'We shall have it packed in oil-paper here, Hoong, then take it down to the tribunal in my palankeen. There we must have the amount verified at once, and in the presence of reliable witnesses.'

The judge fell silent. Crossing his arms in his wide sleeves, he looked up at the perfectly symmetrical silhouette of the temple, outlined against the evening sky. The sergeant tugged pensively at his thin goatee, his right elbow in his cupped left hand. After a long while, he said:

'This afternoon Your Honour placed Yang's card on top of that of Lee Ko. Did you already suspect that Yang was impersonating the painter?'

Judge Dee looked round at him.

'Yes, I did, Hoong. It struck me that, although the self-styled painter was able to conduct an intelligent conversation about the theory of pictorial art—and any student of literature is capable of doing that—he could not paint on short notice the picture I had ordered. His excuses were pure nonsense. A painter who could do the splendid work we saw in the atelier would have set to work at once on a picture of the border scenery, a subject he was thoroughly familiar with and for which I would have paid a good price. And I have never heard from my Third Lady that good paper is difficult to obtain here in Lan-fang. Also, when I visited him unexpectedly, together with Ma Joong, I noticed that the paint in the platters had dried out and was covered with dust, proving they hadn't been used for a day or so. His telling us that Yang was on a spree confirmed my doubts, although I had to admit that Ma Joong had a point when he said that innkeepers often give spurious information. Finally, Hoong, there was this curious outburst of violence of the past three days. Three people killed, and two murderous attacks on Ma Joong! I had the distinct feeling that a new element had entered the case, that an entirely new person was after the gold, a man who had a compelling reason for trying to leave here as soon as possible. That supported my theory of an impersonation. For, although both the painter and Yang were known for their erratic habits, there was still the risk of a shopkeeper or trades-man of their neighbourhood asking awkward questions. After the experiment with the trap door had proved that Mr and Mrs Woo, Lee Mai and the Abbess were innocent, I knew that Yang Mou-te was our man.'

The sergeant nodded.

'It would have taken superhuman self-restraint not to jump back knowing one was standing on a trap door that was about to open on a crypt twenty feet deep!'

'Exactly. Well, a capricious fate willed that neither Yang nor Lee opened the ebony box, and that I found it and discovered its full import through Spring Cloud's floor-plan of the temple. And it's even more curious that Yang, eager to make up for his failure to produce the painting, tried to make a good impression on me by telling me how he got that ebony box—never sus-pecting what weighty consequences that simple gesture would have! A strange case, Hoong. A very strange case indeed!'

The judge shook his head and began to caress his long side whiskers.

Sergeant Hoong gave him a sideways glance. After some hesitation, he cleared his throat and said, 'You have explained everything, sir. Except the phantom.'

Judge Dee came out of his reverie. Looking hard at the sergeant, he said slowly, 'The Phantom of the Temple shall never stalk about here again, Hoong. The strange ties, mystic and otherwise, that bound it to this old temple have been severed. For good. Ha, there we have Ma Joong!' Seeing the tall man's dejected face, the judge asked, alarmed, 'Has Fang taken a turn for the worse?'

'Oh no, sir. I just had a look at him, after I had seen the Abbess home. He's doing fine.'

Judge Dee got up. 'Good. There's a lot of work to be done, Ma Joong. We shall go back to the hall and open the crypt. The constables will be here soon with everything needed for hauling up the two corpses and the gold.'

The judge crossed the yard, his two lieutenants following behind.

Ma Joong heaved a deep sigh. 'Women,' he told the sergeant sombrely, 'are fickle creatures.'

'So they say,' the sergeant replied absent-mindedly.

Ma Joong laid his large hand on his arm. 'Youth seeks youth, sergeant. One lives and learns. But it hurts.'

Sergeant Hoong suddenly remembered the fond look the wounded young constable had given Spring Cloud, and her sudden blush. So he just nodded and quickly walked on.

XXI

It was late in the night by the time Judge Dee had finished the most urgent business resulting from the discovery in the deserted temple. The Treasurer's gold had been carefully weighed and its value assessed, in the presence of four witnesses: four of the notables of Lanfang, hastily summoned to the tribunal. Then the fifty gold bars had been made into five sealed parcels and placed in the large safe in the chancery. Six soldiers would stand guard there all through the night. In the morning Ma Joong would take the gold to the prefecture, accompanied by a unit of mounted military police. The prefect would see to it that the gold was forwarded to the Imperial capital.

When the judge had signed and sealed his report to the prefect, he told Sergeant Hoong to put it in a large official envelope. He went to the wash-stand in the corner, and rubbed his face and neck with a towel dipped in the cold water.

'We have a complete case,' he told the sergeant. 'I don't expect Yang will bring forward any new facts when I hear him in court tomorrow morning. I think he'll limit himself to a formal confession of having instigated the murder of Lee Ko, of having himself murdered Seng-san, and having subsequently severed their heads in order to be able to switch the bodies and hide the tattooed clue to the temple and the gold. He'll also confess to the murder of the constable. He fully realizes he's done for, and that nothing will save him from being executed in the severest way known to the law. When he was being locked up in his cell, he seemed utterly calm and resigned to his fate.'

The judge paused. He took a comb from his sleeve and began to comb his beard and whiskers. Giving the sergeant a grave look, he resumed, 'Yet you'll realize, Hoong, that there are still a few loose ends to be tied up. I don't think I shall have to take any further legal action, but it is my duty to make sure. Ma Joong is still busy up in the deserted temple, supervising the cleaning of the crypt. If you aren't too tired, Hoong, I would like you to go with me when I make a call down town.'

'I would like very much to accompany you, sir,' the sergeant said quietly. 'For I don't think it'll be a very pleasant call.'

Judge Dee smiled wanly. How well his old friend always gauged his mood!

'Thank you, Hoong. We'll go as we are, and leave the tribunal by the back door. We'll hire a sedan chair in the street.'

The bearers put the chair down in front of the Temple of the War God. While the judge was paying them off, Sergeant Hoong made inquiries from two loafers who were sitting on the broad stone steps of the temple gate. He asked the way to a cheap brothel, housed in an old military barrack. They told him, with a contemptuous sneer.

Together they walked on to the poor quarter. A street urchin took them to the barrack on the corner of the crooked lane. Now all the windows of the ramshackle wooden building were open. Heavily made-up women were leaning out. Fanning themselves with fans of gaudy silk, they shouted inviting remarks at the passers-by. But the men in the street didn't heed them. Standing about in small groups, they were discussing the happenings in the deserted temple. The coolies and beggars who had accompanied Judge Dee's cortège had rushed back to the city to tell the news.

Judge Dee recognized the barred arch window Ma Joong had described, and the low, dark door-opening farther on. It reminded the judge of the entrance to a tomb.

He descended the steep steps, followed by Sergeant Hoong.

After the noise in the street outside, the stillness that reigned in the cellar was uncanny. The old man in black was sitting huddled up in his window, his head resting on the bamboo stick across his knees. In the rear the candle shone on the large head of the King, cradled on his folded arms. He seemed to be sleeping.

When Judge Dee stepped up to the table, there came a fluttering sound from above, and a thin voice screamed:

'A beard, Monk! A beard! Wake up!'

The stick swept down in a threatening curve.

'Be quiet, you!' Judge Dee barked at the bald man. 'I am the magistrate.'

The man in the window shrank. He pressed his frail body against the iron bars, in a dead fright.

The King had raised his head from the table. He pointed at the stool in front.

'Sit down, judge. You must be tired, for I am told you had a heavy night.'

Judge Dee took the bamboo stool. Sergeant Hoong

came to stand behind him. Silently the judge took in the giant's broad, grooved face, the still eyes, the high forehead. Then his eyes strayed to the table-top, covered with intricate carved designs. He heaved a sigh and rubbed his stiff knees. He had been on his feet the entire night.

'Well, what can I do for you?' the other asked in his deep voice.

'You can help me with some expert advice, Monk,' the judge replied quietly. 'You aren't called the Monk for nothing, are you? You were a real monk, once. Of the Temple of the Purple Clouds. Long ago, when the esoteric ritual was still being practised there. And, after the authorities had the temple vacated, you built the Hermitage. You and one priestess. Therefore I consider you an expert on temples, Monk.'

The giant nodded slowly.

'Yes, judge, those who call you an exceedingly clever man are right. You need no advice, judge, none whatsoever. And certainly not from me.'

'I do. On a minor detail, you see. Aren't the airshafts of a crypt under a temple always provided with gratings? To prevent rats from entering them? I don't mention rabbits, of course.'

The King sat very still. His immensely broad shoulders sagged still further. Looking up at the judge from under the ragged fringe of his long grey eyebrows, he muttered, 'So you know. Yes, you are clever, judge. I have said it before, and I'll say it again!'

'You forgot about the gratings, Monk, but you also made a more serious mistake. The wording of the message you put in the box was all wrong. Why should a girl who is dying from hunger and thirst add *the year* to the date of her message? I saw at once that it was utterly wrong. And then, after I had understood that the jade disc on the box was intended to hint at the place where she allegedly was kept captive, I knew for certain that the entire message was a hoax. Granted that she might have found such an ebony box among the litter in the crypt, and granted that she had a tinderbox to light one of the old candles there, nobody in his senses would ever believe that a frantic girl who feels that her life is ebbing away would think up such an elaborate puzzle.' Pointing at the table-top, he resumed: 'Such a puzzle would rather emanate from the warped brain of someone who sits brooding over magic figures, for days on end.'

'Why should I fake messages from dying girls, judge?'

'In order to blackmail her murderer. It was one of your beggars, Monk, who took the ebony box to Lee Ko, with instructions to say that it had been found near a rabbit hole, on the slope behind the temple. The rabbit hole would suggest to the murderer an airshaft, and warn him that the sender of the box knew everything. That his foul deed had been discovered because Miss Jade had not been killed by her fall into the crypt, and had written that message in her last moments with her own blood, then got it outside by throwing it down the airshaft. To me, Monk, it suggested another, very important fact. Namely, that the sender of the box knew that the murderer, after he had pushed Miss Jade into the crypt, had closed the trap door at once, without verifying whether the fall had killed her. Answer me, Monk. How did you know that?'

The other did not reply at once. He seemed lost in thought. When he spoke up at last, his voice was utterly weary.

'Tala is dead, and I am a dying man. Why shouldn't

I tell you, judge? Tala was in the temple, that night of the tenth. She was bound by mystic ties to the central spot in the hall, the holy lotus flower, the eternal symbol of the source of life, hallowed by continuous sacrifice. Every night when there was a full moon she went there, to burn the sacred wood. Tala saw that young woman enter the hall, and followed her. Lee Ko was standing by the open crypt, and Tala saw him push the girl inside and close the trap door. Tala told me. She didn't ask Lee why he had thrown her into the crypt. Tala never asked questions.'

'She did yesterday,' the judge said. 'When my lieutenant went to see her, she asked her god about the girl, after she had learned from my lieutenant that her name had been Jade. The answer was that Jade had died on the tenth, and of a broken neck. That was true, for I examined her dead body tonight. That god of Tala's also told her that she herself would die today. And that came true also.'

The Monk slowly shook his large head.

'Tala was strong, judge. Stronger than I, and Lee, and Yang. But her god was stronger than her. She was wedded to him by the strange rites that transcend the boundary between life and death. You asked about my faked message, judge. I sent it to Lee to frighten him. Frighten him into giving me that gold. So that I could take Tala away from him. Next to her god, she belonged to me.

'The next day I sent Cross-eye, my old henchman in the window up there, to Lee's place. To summon him to my cellar. But Lee apparently hadn't understood, for he never came.'

'You shouldn't have covered the box with dried mud, Monk. Yang came to the door and bought the box, but

199

neither he nor Lee ever gave it a second look. Lee sold it, together with some other rubbish, to a curio-dealer. And I bought it from him. At first . . .'

The other raised his large hand.

'Enough of that accursed box, judge. Let's talk about Lee. Tala threw him away, as one throws away a piece of sugar cane, chewed dry. And she took Yang. The other day she came to see me. Told me you were after her, but that it didn't matter. Yang knew now where the gold was, and he had killed Lee, and Lee's helper, Seng-san. She would flee with Yang over the border. It was time, for her people were turning against her, and her god had told her she was about to die, join him for ever. But she didn't believe him, this time. She laughed when she said that. And now she's dead. The gods have the last laugh, judge. Always.' He stared at nothing, his eyes vacant. Suddenly he darted a quick glance at the judge and asked: 'What did you do with her dead body?'

'I had it cremated, and the ashes scattered. That was her last wish.'

The other lifted his big hands in a hopeless gesture.

'That means I have lost her. For ever. The wind will blow her ashes over the plain, and they'll change into a white witch, rushing through the air, white and naked on her black steed, by the side of the red god, her master. They'll ride the gale together when it comes raging over the desert, and when the Tartars hear her scream they'll cower in their tents and say their prayers. You should've buried her ashes, Judge.'

'The rule is,' Judge Dee said dryly, 'that the ashes of a person who leaves no known relatives are scattered.'

'You don't believe the things I told you, do you, judge?'

'I neither believe nor disbelieve them. You asked a

futile question, Monk. Tell me, where did the gold in the temple come from?'

'I don't know. Tala knew, but she never told me. Someone must have hidden it there, last year. In my time it wasn't there.'

'I see. Did Lee Ko meet Tala in the temple?'

For a long time the Monk remained silent. His large head sunk, he aimlessly traced with his finger the incised designs on the table-top. At last he spoke: 'Lee was a learned man and a great artist. But he wanted to know too much, far too much. There are things that even a wise man like you had better not know, judge. Therefore I shall tell you only this. Twenty years ago, when I was forty and Tala twenty, we were the high priest and high priestess of the Temple of the Purple Clouds. When, five years later, the authorities closed down the temple, we feigned to forswear the creed, and continued to practise it in secret, in the Hermitage. For we were adepts, versed in all the mysteries. We knew much about what people for want of better words call the beginning and the end of the spark of life. We knew too much. But we didn't know, judge, that man is bound to travel in circles, always. Just when you think you have arrived at the end, about to reach the ultimate mystery, you suddenly find yourself right back where you started. Tala, the high priestess, who knew all the secrets, fell in love with Lee Ko. And she left me.'

Suddenly he laughed. It echoed hollowly in the empty cellar. The old man in the window began to hop to and fro. The Monk checked himself. He said sombrely: 'You didn't laugh, judge. You are right. For the biggest laugh is yet to come. You'd think that I, the high priest of esoteric love, would just shrug at her folly, and go my way, wouldn't you? No. When she was moving from

201

the Hermitage to the city, I begged her not to leave me, judge! Begged her!' With a superhuman effort he raised himself on his muscular arms and shouted: 'Laugh now, judge! Laugh at me, I tell you!'

Judge Dee met his haunted eyes levelly. 'I don't know how Tala felt about you, Monk. I do know, however, that she still loved her daughter. Last night she was luring my lieutenant to the spot behind the temple where Yang would kill him, letting the top of the crumbling wall crush him. But at the very last moment, she suddenly saw your daughter coming up behind him, and she raised her arms in alarm. That frantic gesture frightened my lieutenant. He halted in his steps, and that saved his life.'

The Monk glanced away.

'I had hoped,' he said in a low voice, 'that Tala would discard Yang in the same manner as she had discarded Lee. Abandon Yang, as soon as he had got the gold. I also hoped I would then be able to wean her away from her terrible god. For although the spark of life has died in me, I am still familiar with the unnamed rites, and I still know the unutterable spells.' He heaved a deep sigh that swelled his broad chest. 'Yes, I had hoped to free her from her bonds, and take her and our daughter over the border, to our own people. To ride over the wide plain again! To ride on and on, for days on end, in the clean, crisp air of the desert!'

'I remember,' Judge Dee said slowly, 'that I told Yang that the horse that breaks loose from the team will roam over the plain, free and untrammelled. But the day will come when it grows lonely and tired. Then it finds itself all alone and lost—the track effaced by the wind, and the chariot vanished beyond the horizon.'

The Monk, lost in thought, did not seem to have heard

202

him. When he spoke again, his voice was very soft.

'Without her god, Tala would have shrunk to an empty shell, just like me. For although the gods let us spend freely all we want to spend, they never give any of it back. But even two empty, old people who love each other can at least wait for death together. Now that I have lost Tala, I shall have to wait alone. It won't be too long.' His voice had become so low as to be hardly audible. He raised his head, and whispered hoarsely, 'It's getting late, judge. You'd better go. Unless you think you should take action against me, or . . . or take my testimony . . .'

The judge rose. He shook his head and said, 'My case is complete, Monk. There is nothing to be done, nothing to be said. Not any more. Goodbye.'

He went to the staircase, followed by Sergeant Hoong. The small old man squatting in the window had drawn the tattered black robe close to him, his shoulders hunched, his bald head drawn in. A ruffled crow gone to roost.

POSTSCRIPT

Judge Dee was a historical person who lived from 630 to 700 A.D., during the Tang dynasty. Besides earning fame as a great detective, he was also a brilliant statesman who, in the second half of his career, played an important role in China's internal and foreign policy. The adventures related here, however, are entirely fictitious, and the Lan-fang district, where the events described in this novel are supposed to have occurred, is wholly imaginary.

The new, esoteric sect of Buddhism frequently referred to is Tantrism, flourishing at that time in India and abroad, cf. Appendix I of my book *Sexual Life in Ancient China, a preliminary survey of Chinese sex and society from c. 1500 B.C. till 1644 A.D.* (E. J. Brill, Leiden, 1961).

In Judge Dee's time the Chinese did not wear pigtails; that custom was imposed on them after 1644 A.D., when the Manchus had conquered China. Before that date they let their hair grow long, and did it up in a top-knot. They wore caps both inside and outside the house, and both men and women dressed in wide, long-sleeved robes resembling the Japanese *kimono*—which is, in fact, derived from the Chinese Tang costume. Only the military, and low-class people, wore short dresses that showed the wide trousers and leggings. Tea, rice wine and various kinds of strong liquor were the national beverages. Tobacco and opium were introduced into China only many centuries later.

ROBERT VAN GULIK